CREEPER
And
THE NINE MISCHIEVOUS
Dandy Ahuruonye

CREEPERELLA AND THE NINE MISCHIEVOUS MONSTERS 3

UK | USA | Canada | Ireland | Australia | India | New Zealand | South Africa | Japan | China | Nigeria
De Juvenyles is part of the dandyahuruonyebooks.com whose details can be found at
https://dandyahuruonye.wordpress.com & https://www.amazon.com/author/dandyahuruonye
Dandyahuruonyebooks, Tallaght, Dublin, Ireland.
This edition was published in 2024; No 0020
Copyright © Dandy Ahuruonye, 2014 – 2024

The story, all names, characters and incidents portrayed in this novel are fictitious. No identification with actual persons, places, buildings or products is intended or should be inferred.

The moral rights of the author and illustrator have been asserted.

The author's official representative globally is dandyahuruonyebooks.com

A CIP catalogue record for this book from the British Library, The Library of Congress, & Bibliothèque Nationale de France is pending.

All correspondence should be directed to:
dandyahuruonyebooks@gmail.com
All rights reserved.

Myths about monsters are often ignored or dismissed. Always beware of monsters who don't ask twice.

CREDITS

Groccofly—Dandy Ahuruonye
Grass Fart in Donegal Bay—Dandy Ahuruonye
The Doghouse of Calabarry—Dandy Ahuruonye
The Adventures of Groccolli—Dandy Ahuruonye
The Cute Children of Madugascar—Dandy Ahuruonye
Childhood Favourites—Helen Oxenbury & Eugene Trivizas
Samankwe & the Highway Robbers—Cyprian Ekwensi
In Search of Greener Pastures—Dandy Ahuruonye
Waka—Dandy Ahuruonye
Bing Search Engine
Microsoft Copilot
The best way to deal with fearsome monsters is to ride them.

Dandy Ahaoma Ahuruonye personally wrote and published this original story.

CREEPERELLA AND THE NINE MISCHIEVOUS MONSTERS 7

CREEPERELLA
And
THE NINE MISCHIEVOUS MONSTERS
Dandy Ahuruonye

OUTLINE

Welcome, dear reader, to the wild and wacky world of Creeperella and her merry band of mischievous monsters. This isn't just any ordinary tale of monsters lurking in the dark corners; oh no, this is a story brimming with laughter, adventure, and a sprinkle of sheer madness.

Nestled in the heart of the mysterious Misty Mountains, Creeperella and her eclectic crew of nine monsters have made quite a name for themselves. Our star, Creeperella, is a master of drama, with her vine-like hair and shape-shifting abilities, always ready to add a bit of flair to any situation. Whether she's rolling her eyes at Gigglefang's antics or tripping over her own feet while planning pranks, Creeperella ensures there's never a dull moment.

But Creeperella isn't the only showstopper here. Let me introduce you to the gang. First, we have Nyaka, the fur-changing diva, with a profound dislike for vets. With her ever-changing colours and fiercely independent streak, Nyaka is a walking, talking mood ring. Then there's Gigglefang, the furry creature with oversized fangs, and a laugh so infectious it could make a grumpy goblin giggle.

And who could forget the ever-clumsy Blunderbuss? This gentle giant may trip over rocks and knock over obstacles, but his heart is as big as his feet. Adding to the mix is Wobblewomp, the gooey blob who loves dancing and bouncy castles, and the lightning-fast Zippityzap, always leaving a trail of sparks in his wake.

We also have Snickerdoodle, the tiny winged trickster with a fondness for sparkling sugar cubes, and Fizzlebop, the bubbly monster with a body made of fizzy soda. His biggest fear? Flat drinks, naturally. Rounding out the crew is Mumblegrumble, the grumpy monster with a secret love for fun, and Tiddlywink, the bold little adventurer who can shrink and grow at will. And what about a monster who could polish off a whole roast dragon, a bucket of bugs, and a tank of slime in one sitting? These are the moments memories are made of.

Each chapter of "Creeperella and Nine Mischievous Monsters" takes you on a whirlwind journey through the lives of these delightful creatures. From Nyaka's vet aversion and Gigglefang's legendary pranks to Blunderbuss's hilarious mishaps, this book is packed with laughter, surprises, and a lot of heart.

Prepare to be enchanted by the escapades of Grumble the Grumbler, a master of the art of moaning and groaning, whose love for food rivals even the most dedicated gourmands. From his grand feasts to the heroic rescue of Fluffins from the clutches of the wicked Hagatha, Grumble's tales are sure to tickle your taste buds and your funny bone.

Join us as we dive into the chaotic yet heart-warming world of Creeperella and her quirky companions. Whether it's a puddle-jumping contest on a rainy day or a daring adventure to uncover hidden treasures, one thing's for sure – with this motley crew, there's never a dull moment. So please sit back, relax, and get ready to laugh out loud as you embark on this unforgettable journey with Creeperella and her nine mischievous monsters.

CREEPERELLA AND THE NINE MISCHIEVOUS MONSTERS

"Creeperella and Nine Mischievous Monsters" Deserves a Spot on Your Bookshelf.

Dear parents, grandparents, and book-loving creatures of all ages, gather 'round for an important announcement! Allow me to introduce you to the most delightful, side-splittingly funny book you'll ever have the pleasure of reading this year: "Creeperella and Nine Mischievous Monsters." Why should you buy this book, you ask? Well, let's dive right in, shall we? First off, imagine a world where bedtime stories aren't a chore but an absolute delight. That's exactly what you'll get with Creeperella and her band of quirky companions. This book is the perfect remedy for the bedtime blues, transforming yawns into giggles and "just one more chapter" please into the norm.

For the kids, it's like opening a portal to a land of endless fun and adventure. Each character is more loveable and hilariously unpredictable than the last. Take Creeperella, for example. With her dramatic sighs and vine-like hair, she's always up to something, whether it's plotting pranks or rolling her eyes at Gigglefang's never-ending antics. Or how about the irresistible Monster Nyaka, the fur-changing diva with a vet aversion so intense it could rival a cat's dislike for water?

But let's not forget the educational angle. Yes, you heard that right. Through their wild adventures, your little ones will learn valuable lessons about bravery, friendship, and the importance of a good laugh. Each page is a treasure trove of teachable moments wrapped in the most entertaining package you could imagine. Parents, you'll find yourself chuckling along with your kids. The witty banter and laugh-out-loud situations are written with a charm that appeals to both young and old. This isn't just a book for children; it's a packaged family experience. You might even catch yourself sneaking a read after the kids have hit the sack. And who could blame you? With characters like Blunderbuss, the clumsy giant with a heart of gold, and Fizzlebop, the bubbly monster whose biggest fear is flat drinks, it's impossible to resist.

Now, just picture this: a rainy afternoon, the sound of laughter echoing through your home as you and your little ones embark on an adventure with Zippityzap, the lightning-fast monster, or join Snickerdoodle, the tiny winged trickster, in her latest escapade. And what about a monster who could polish off a whole roast dragon, a bucket of bugs, and a tank of slime in one sitting? These are the moments memories are made of.

So, why should you buy "Creeperella and Nine Mischievous Monsters"? Because it's not just a book; it's an invitation to a world of fun, absolute chaos, laughter, and heart-warming adventures. It's a chance to bond with your kids over stories that are as educational as they are entertaining. And most importantly, it's a guarantee that bedtime will never be the same again.

Go on, add a dash of monster mischief to your bookshelf. Trust me, you'll be glad you did. Your kids will thank you, and you might just find yourself enjoying it even more than they do...!

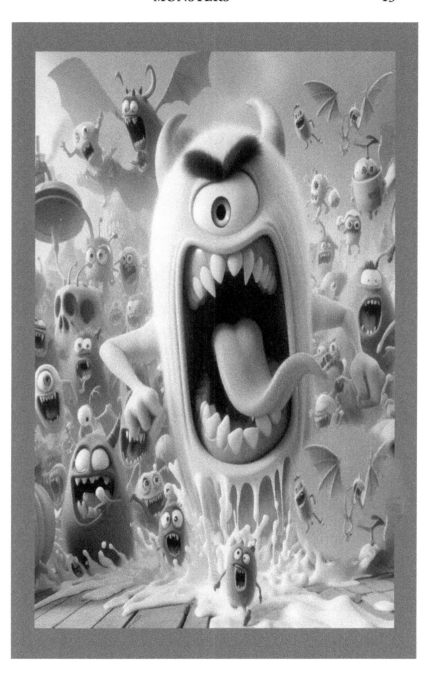

1: MONSTERS' PROFILES

Creeperella: Well, hello there, folks! Welcome to the wacky world of Creeperella, the girl with vine-like hair who's always getting herself into a spot of bother. You see, Creeperella's not your average gal. She's got a knack for turning ordinary situations into extraordinary adventures. And her hair? Well, let's just say it's got a mind of its own. One minute, it's a flowing waterfall of green; the next, it's a tangled mess that could trip up a yeti. But don't worry, Creeperella's always got a smile on her face, even when her hair is in knots.

Characteristics: A chill girl with vine-like hair. Personality: Sweet, curious, and a bit clumsy. Quirk: Her hair can grow and shrink at will, often surprising her friends and family. Likes: Gardening, playing with her pet snail, and reading Groccolli tales, especially those with strong female protagonists. Dislikes: Bugs, being called "creepy," and losing her glasses, which are essential for her to read and see the world clearly. Weaknesses: Scared of heights and loud noises, which can startle her and make her feel overwhelmed. Strengths: Good at problem-solving and caring for others, always ready to lend a helping hand. Preferred Food: Apple pie with a side of worms, a peculiar combination that she finds surprisingly delicious.

Gooey Louie

Meet Gooey Louie, the blob of blue goo who's always up to no good. Louie's a bit of a prankster, you see, and he loves nothing more

CREEPERELLA AND THE NINE MISCHIEVOUS MONSTERS

than to get his friends and family all gooey and sticky. But don't be fooled by his mischievous grin—Louie's actually a pretty nice guy once you get to know him. He just can't help himself when it comes to a good joke. Gooey also has googly eyes and a playful personality. He can bounce and stretch like a rubber band, making him incredibly flexible and difficult to catch. Louie loves eating candy and watching cartoons. His favourite hiding spot is under the bed, where he can surprise his friends with a gooey hug. Just don't bring out the vacuum cleaner—it's one of his biggest fears!

Characteristics: A blob of blue goo with googly eyes. Personality: Playful, mischievous, and a bit messy, always up to some sort of prank or mischief.

Quirk: He can bounce and stretch like a rubber band, making him incredibly flexible and difficult to catch. Likes: Playing pranks, eating candy, and watching cartoons, especially those featuring silly and goofy characters. Dislikes: Baths, being stuck in a jar, and losing his favourite toy, a squeaky rubber duck named "Quacky." Weaknesses: Afraid of vacuum cleaners and sharp objects, which can easily pop him or deflate him. Strengths: Good at hiding and escaping, often leaving his friends and family searching for him. Preferred Food: Jellybeans and chocolate pudding, which he enjoys slurping up with his gooey tongue.

Giggles the Goblin

Giggles is a small, green goblin with a laugh so big it could fill an entire cavern. He's always up for a good time and loves playing pranks on his friends. Whether it's filling Giggles the Goblin's cave with feathers or setting up tickle traps around the campfire, Giggles' antics are sure to leave you in fits of laughter. Just watch out for his giggle-inducing tricks! He's the funniest creature in all of Monsterland. He's got a laugh that could shake the very foundations of the earth, and he's always got a wicked joke up his sleeve. But Giggles isn't just a comedian—he's also a bit of a troublemaker. He loves to play pranks on his friends and family, and he's always getting himself into all sorts of scrapes. But no matter what, Giggles always manages to come out smelling like roses, and with a belly full of laughter.

Characteristics: A small, green goblin with a big laugh. Personality: Happy-go-lucky, silly, and a bit forgetful, always laughing and joking around. Quirk: He can turn invisible when he laughs, making him a master of hide-and-seek. Likes: Telling jokes, playing tag, and eating marshmallows, which he loves to roast over a campfire. Dislikes: Being tickled, doing homework, and going to bed early, preferring to stay up late and have fun. Weaknesses: Easily distracted and sometimes gets lost, often wandering off and forgetting where he is. Strengths: Good at making friends and cheering people up, always bringing a smile to everyone's face. Preferred Food: Pizza with extra cheese and a side of pickles, a strange combination that he finds incredibly tasty.

Sneezy the Sniffler: Sneezy is the world's greatest detective Sniffler. He's got a nose that can sniff out anything, from a missing sock to a stolen treasure. But Sneezy isn't just a detective—he's also a bit of a hypochondriac. He's always convinced that he's got some terrible illness and constantly sniffs for symptoms. However, there is no need to worry, as Sneezy tends to exaggerate and overreact to situations. He's quite healthy and always happy to help out his friends and family, even if it means getting his nose dirty.

Characteristics: A tiny, pink creature with a long, floppy nose. Personality: Curious, polite, and a bit shy, always sniffing out new adventures. Quirk: He can smell anything from a mile away, making him a master detective of sorts. Likes: Exploring, collecting treasures, and reading adventure stories, especially those with pirates and treasure maps. Dislikes: Being tickled, getting his nose dirty, and being called "smelly," which he finds incredibly offensive. Weaknesses: Scared of spiders and heights, which can make him freeze up and refuse to move. Strengths: Good at finding lost things and solving mysteries, using his keen sense of smell to track down clues. Preferred Food: Honey and berries, which he enjoys slurping up with his long, floppy nose.

Fizzy the Fizzler

Fizzy the Fizzler is the most energetic creature in all of Monsterland. He's always bouncing around, fizzing and popping like a soda can. But Fizzy's not just a ball of energy—he's also a bit of a klutz. He's always tripping over his own feet and bumping into things that aren't even there, but it's all part of his charm. Fizzy, who is a lovable chap, has the wonderful ability to brighten up your day with his bubbly personality, and he is always there for you.

Characteristics: A bubbly, yellow creature with a fizzy personality. Personality: Energetic, excitable, and a bit clumsy, always on the go and full of energy. Quirk: He can fizz and pop like a soda, making him a walking carbonation machine. Likes: Playing sports, swimming, and eating candy, especially sour gummy worms and lollipops. Dislikes: Being quiet, sitting still, and losing his ball, which he cherishes more than anything. Weaknesses: Afraid of water balloons and thunderstorms, which can scare him and make him fizz uncontrollably. Strengths: Good at running and jumping, always the first to reach the finish line in any race. Preferred Food: Root beer floats and gummy bears, which he loves to combine for a fizzy and sweet treat.

Nibbles the Nibbler

Nibbles the Nibbler is the hungriest creature in all of Monsterland. He's always on the lookout for his next meal, and he's not afraid to eat anything, no matter how gross or disgusting. But Nibbles isn't just a glutton—he's also a bit of a thief. He's always trying to steal food from his friends and family, and he's got a knack for getting into trouble. But despite his greedy ways, Nibbles is actually a pretty nice guy. He's just got a weakness for a good meal.

Characteristics: A tiny, brown creature with sharp teeth. Personality: Hungry, mischievous, and a bit greedy, always on the lookout for his next meal. Quirk: He can eat anything, even rocks and metal, making him a living garbage disposal. Likes: Eating, playing hide-and-seek, and watching cartoons about food, especially those featuring delicious-looking dishes. Dislikes: Sharing his food, being told "no," and going on diets, which he finds incredibly unfair. Weaknesses: Afraid of dentists and toothaches, which can make him squirm and cry. Strengths: Good at chewing and digging, always able to find a way to get into any locked container. Preferred Food: Anything and everything! From pizza to pickles, chocolate to cheese, Nibbles loves it all.

Sleepy the Snoozer: Sleepy the Snoozer is the laziest creature in all of Monsterland. He's always on the lookout for a good nap, and he's not afraid to sleep anywhere, anytime. But Sleepy isn't just a lazybones—he's also a bit of a grump. He's always complaining and moaning about something, and he's not afraid to let you know how much he hates doing anything. But don't let Sleepy's grumpy exterior fool you—he's actually a pretty sweet guy once you get to know him. He just needs a lot of sleep.

Characteristics: A big, blue creature with a sleepy expression. Personality: Lazy, peaceful, and a bit grumpy, always looking for a good nap. Quirk: He can sleep anywhere, anytime, even in the most uncomfortable positions. Likes: Napping, watching clouds, and eating ice cream, especially the chocolate chip flavour. Dislikes: Being woken up, doing chores, and going outside, preferring to stay indoors and relax. Weaknesses: Afraid of loud noises and bright lights, which can disrupt his sleep and put him in a bad mood.

CREEPERELLA AND THE NINE MISCHIEVOUS MONSTERS

Strengths: Good at relaxing and taking it easy, always able to find a comfortable spot to rest. Preferred Food: Pancakes with syrup and a side of bacon, a classic breakfast that he loves to savour.

Squishy the Squisher

Squishy the Squisher is the messiest creature in all of Monsterland. He's always covered in goo and slime, and he's always leaving a trail of destruction wherever he goes. But Squishy isn't just a messy monster—he's also a bit of a prankster. He loves to play tricks on his friends and family, and he's always getting himself into trouble. But Squishy's a lovable character, and he's always there for a hug, even if he's a bit sticky.

Characteristics: A squishy, green creature with a gooey texture. Personality: Playful, messy, and a bit sticky, always getting into trouble with his sticky fingers. Quirk: He can squish and squelch like a mud puddle, making him incredibly difficult to catch. Likes: Playing in the mud, making messes, and eating slime, which he finds incredibly delicious. Dislikes: Baths, being cleaned up, and losing his favourite toy, a squeaky rubber duck named "Quacky." Weaknesses: Afraid of vacuum cleaners and sharp objects, which can easily pop him or deflate him. Strengths: Good at hiding and escaping, often leaving his friends and family searching for him. Preferred Food: Jellybeans and chocolate pudding, which he enjoys slurping up with his gooey tongue.

Twinkle the Twirler

Twinkle the Twirler is the most sparkly creature in all of Monsterland. She's always covered in glitter and rainbows, and she's always spinning and twirling around. But Twinkle isn't just a pretty face—she's also a bit of a daydreamer. She's always lost in her own little world, and she's not always paying attention to what's going on around her. But Twinkle's a lovable character, and she's always there to brighten up your day with her sparkly personality.

Characteristics: A sparkling, pink creature with a twirling personality. Personality: Energetic, playful, and a bit dizzy, always spinning and twirling around. Quirk: She can spin and twirl like a top, making her a human tornado of sorts. Likes: Dancing, playing games, and eating candy, especially cotton candy and lollipops. Dislikes: Being still and losing her favourite toy, a sparkly unicorn horn. Weaknesses: Afraid of heights and getting dizzy, which can sometimes make her lose her balance. Strengths: Good at dancing and being the centre of attention, always the life of the party. Preferred Food: Cotton candy and lollipops, which she loves to twirl around in her mouth.

Grumble the Grumbler

Grumble the Grumbler is the grumpiest creature in all of Monsterland. He's always complaining and moaning about something, and he's not afraid to let you know how much he hates everything. But Grumble isn't just a grumpy old monster—he's also a bit of a know-it-all. He thinks he knows everything, and he's always trying to correct people. But Grumble's a lovable character, in his own grumpy way. And you can always count on him to tell you the truth, no matter how unpleasant it might be.

Characteristics: A grumpy, grey creature with a frown. Personality: Moody, grumpy, and a bit sarcastic, always complaining and finding fault with everything. Quirk: He can grumble and complain about anything, from the weather to the food to the other monsters. Likes: Being alone, watching TV, and eating pizza, especially with extra cheese and pepperoni. Dislikes: Being happy, doing chores, and going outside, preferring to stay indoors and grumble. Weaknesses: Afraid of surprises and change, which can throw him off and make him even grumpier. Strengths: Good at being grumpy and complaining, always finding something to be unhappy about. Preferred Food: Pizza with extra cheese and a side of pickles, a classic comfort food that he enjoys even when he's in a bad mood.

CREEPERELLA AND THE NINE MISCHIEVOUS MONSTERS

2: OTHER MONSTERS

Let's take a sneak peek at some other delightful monsters you might encounter along the way:

Monster Nyaka: Nyaka is a tall, gangly monster with fur that changes colour based on her mood. She's fiercely independent and has a deep-seated fear of vets, so she chooses her vet and pays for her own treatments. Nyaka's inventive mind has allowed her to replicate the genius of her favourite vet, who created wonders like the Fur-Fluffer and the Dreamcatcher 3000. Her adventures are filled with ingenuity and heart, making her a truly unforgettable character.

Quibblequack: Quibblequack is the new kid on the block, and he's as unusual as they come. With feathers instead of fur and a beak that looks like it belongs on a duck, Quibblequack is a master of mischief. His pranks, like filling Blunderbuss's cave with helium balloons or replacing Creeperella's pen ink with invisible ink, are legendary. But beneath his mischievous exterior lies a monster just trying to fit in.

Dr Fluffernutter: Dr Fluffernutter is a kind-hearted vet who cares for all the monsters. With her fluffy pink fur and gentle touch, she's the perfect doctor for even the most stubborn patients like Nyaka. Her inventive treatments, like the Tickle-Tonic, are as whimsical as they are effective. Dr Fluffernutter's tea parties are the stuff of legend, filled with laughter, delicious treats, and plenty of tea.

Blunderbuss: Blunderbuss is a clumsy, oversized monster with big feet and a heart of gold. He's always causing accidental trouble, but his friends love him for his kind-hearted nature. Whether he's tripping over rocks or knocking over obstacles, Blunderbuss's antics are sure to bring a smile to your face. Just don't ask him to arrange a party table or navigate a slippery slope – it never ends well!

Wobblewomp: Wobblewomp is a gooey blob that changes shape and colour with his mood. He's easy-going and always in a good mood, bouncing around like a rubber ball. Wobblewomp loves dancing, colourful lights, and bouncy castles. His biggest fear is sharp objects, which can easily pop him. But with his friends by his side, Wobblewomp is always ready for a new adventure.

GIGGLEFANG: GIGGLEFANG is a small, furry creature with oversized fangs and a constant giggle. He can make anyone laugh with a single look, and his jokes are legendary. Gigglefang loves tickle fights, funny faces, and cotton candy clouds. Just don't leave him in silence – he can't stand it!

Snickerdoodle: Snickerdoodle is a tiny, winged creature with a mischievous twinkle in her eyes. She loves playing tricks and causing harmless chaos. Snickerdoodle can turn invisible at will, making her an expert at hide-and-seek. Her favourite food is sparkling sugar cubes, and she's always up for a surprise party. But she dislikes having her ears cleaned and would happily give up her sugar cubes to avoid any ear-cleaning sessions.

Zippityzap: Zippityzap is a lightning-fast creature with electric blue fur. He's energetic and always on the move, leaving a trail of sparks wherever he goes. Zippityzap loves racing, thunderstorms, and neon lights. His biggest weakness is water, which short-circuits him. But with his super speed and agility, Zippityzap is always ready for a new challenge.

Mumblegrumble: Mumblegrumble is a grumpy-looking monster with a perpetual frown. But beneath his grumpy exterior lies a monster who secretly loves fun. Mumblegrumble talks in rhymes when he's happy and enjoys puzzles, rainy days, and cosy blankets. His biggest fear is loud noises, which easily annoy him. But with his clever mind and problem-solving skills, Mumblegrumble is always ready to lend a hand.

Tiddlywink: Tiddlywink is a tiny, colourful monster with a big personality. She's bold and fearless despite her size, and she loves adventure and treasure hunts. Tiddlywink can shrink and grow at will, making her an expert at fitting into small spaces. Her favourite food is miniature cupcakes, and she's always up for a new adventure. However, she hates having her toenails cut.

Fizzlebop: Fizzlebop is a bubbly monster with a body made of fizzy soda. He's always cheerful and makes fizzy sounds when he's excited. Fizzlebop loves soda fountains, bubbles, and fizzy drinks. His biggest fear is flat drinks, which make him lose his fizz. But with his ability to create bubbles of any size, Fizzlebop is always ready to bring a little sparkle to his friends' lives.

Whimsywhirl: Whimsywhirl is a whimsical creature with a body that swirls like a tornado. She's dreamy and imaginative, always lost in her world. Whimsywhirl loves daydreaming, cloud-watching, and spinning. Her biggest weakness is getting dizzy easily, but with her ability to float and fly with the wind, Whimsywhirl is always ready for a new adventure.

Now, that's an ensemble! Each monster brings something special to the table, ready to whisk you away on a whirlwind of fun and fancy.

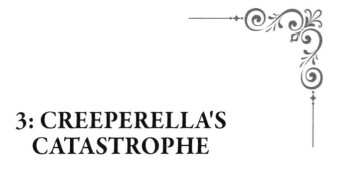

3: CREEPERELLA'S CATASTROPHE

Perchance it was spring; oh, no, it was actually summer, but what mattered so much was that Creeperella was sighing dramatically while rolling her eyes at her rowdy friends.

"Calm down," she pleaded. "I'm just having fun. I'm a harmless monster, minding my own business."

Her appearance shifted frequently. Today, she was short and green, with a mischievous grin. Her vine-like hair trailed behind her, occasionally snagging on things, including her feet. "I'm just different," she insisted. "And a bit green. I know!" She stretched her arms, her skin rippling. "Not so bad. Just a bit of a stretch."

Suddenly, a loud crash echoed through the room. Gigglefang, the small, furry creature with oversized fangs and a constant giggle, had tripped over his own feet and landed in a pile of books. "Oh, Giggles," Creeperella groaned. "You're such a klutz." Gigglefang just laughed. "Hey, it's all part of the fun!"

Just then, Wobblewomp, the blob that changed colour with its mood, bounced into the room, shimmering with a rainbow of colours. "Creeperella!" he exclaimed. "You're going to be late for your date with Blunderbuss!"

Creeperella's face flushed bright red. "What?! No way! I completely forgot!" She scrambled to her feet, her long limbs flailing wildly. "I have to get ready!" As she rushed out of the room, Gigglefang and Wobblewomp exchanged amused glances. "She's such a drama queen," Gigglefang said. "But isn't that why we love her?"

Creeperella burst into her room, her heart pounding. She had been so busy planning her prank on Blunderbuss that she had completely forgotten about their date. She quickly threw on a dress she had stolen from a human closet and grabbed a pair of sparkly shoes. As she was about to leave, she heard a knock at the door. It must be Blunderbuss. She took a deep breath and opened the door. To her surprise, it wasn't Blunderbuss. It was Zippityzap, the lightning-fast creature with electric blue fur.

"Hey, lady Creeperella," he said, grinning. "You look amazing."

Creeperella blushed. "Thanks," she said.

"I was just wondering if you wanted to go for a ride on my lightning bolt," Zippityzap continued.

Creeperella's eyes lit up. "That sounds like fun," she said. She followed Zippityzap outside, where he had parked his lightning bolt. It was a sleek, black machine with streaks of lightning running along its sides. He hopped onto the lightning bolt and held out a hand for her. She hesitated for a moment, then took his hand and climbed aboard. With a roar, Zippityzap took off, soaring through the sky. The wind whipped through Creeperella's hair, and she felt a rush of exhilaration.

"This is amazing," she shouted over the wind.

Zippityzap laughed. "I know, right?"

They flew over the city, the lights below them twinkling like stars. Creeperella felt a sense of peace and freedom that she had never experienced before. After a while, Zippityzap landed on a rooftop. They sat there for a while, watching the city lights.

"This is perfect," Creeperella said.

"I'm glad you like it," Zippityzap replied.

Just then, Creeperella heard a familiar voice.

"Creeperella!" Blunderbuss shouted, running towards them.

Creeperella groaned. She had completely forgotten about her date with him.

"I'm so sorry, Blunderbuss," she said. "I got caught up with this lightning ride."

Blunderbuss just smiled. "It's okay," he said. "I'm glad you're here."

Creeperella smiled back. She knew she was in trouble, but she couldn't help but feel a little excited. She had just had the most amazing adventure with Zippityzap, and she was about to have another one with Blunderbuss.

As Blunderbuss started to walk away, Creeperella grabbed his arm. "Wait," she said. "I have an idea."

She pulled him closer and whispered something in his ear. Blunderbuss's eyes widened.

"Are you sure?"

Creeperella nodded. "Absolutely," she said.

With a mischievous grin, she turned to Zippityzap.

"Ready for some fun?"

Zippityzap grinned back. "You bet," he said.

And so, the three of them set off on a night of adventure, leaving a trail of chaos and dust in their wake.

4: GOOEY LOUIE'S GREAT ESCAPE

Gooey Louie groaned as he pulled himself out of his favourite lazy armchair. He was a blob of blue goo with enormous googly eyes, and he was currently covered in a layer of chocolate pudding. "Alright, alright, I'm coming!" he muttered, his voice a bubbling babble.

"Someone's been snacking again," Creeperella teased, poking him in the side.

Gooey Louie giggled. "Hey, a monster's gotta eat, right?" He stretched his arms out, his gooey body rippling like water. "And what's better than a big bowl of chocolate pudding?"

"Nothing," Creeperella agreed, reaching for a spoonful.

Just then, Snickerdoodle, the tiny winged creature with a mischievous twinkle in her eyes, swooped down from the ceiling. "Hey, Louie," she said, "Wanna play hide-and-seek?"

Gooey Louie's eyes lit up. "You bet!" He turned around and disappeared into a cloud of goo, leaving Creeperella and Snickerdoodle in stitches.

"He's such a kid," Creeperella said.

"That's what I like about him," Snickerdoodle replied.

The two of them started searching for Louie, but he was nowhere to be found. They looked under the beds, behind the curtains, and even in the fridge (to their surprise, he wasn't there).

"Where could he be?" Creeperella wondered.

"He's probably hiding in the bathtub," Snickerdoodle suggested.

They went to the bathroom and looked in the bathtub, but Gooey Louie wasn't there either.

"I don't know where he could have gone," she said, starting to worry.

Just then, they heard a strange noise coming from the basement. They exchanged a worried glance and hurried downstairs. When they reached the basement, they found Louie stuck in a jar of pickles. He was struggling to get out, but the jar was too tight.

"Help!" he yelled.

Creeperella and Snickerdoodle rushed over and tried to pry the jar open, but it wouldn't budge.

"We need to get a bigger jar," Creeperella said.

She ran upstairs and grabbed a bigger jar from the kitchen. When she came back downstairs, she connected the opened end of the two jars together before carefully turning the one containing the goo upside down, allowing the monster to slowly transfer into the new jar due to gravitational pull.

Gooey Louie sighed with relief. "Thanks," he said after regaining his composure.

"You're welcome," Creeperella replied.

As she was about to put the jar down, Gooey Louie squirmed and wriggled until the container popped over and fell sideways. He then jumped out and hugged Creeperella. "You're the best," he said.

Creeperella smiled. "No problem; just don't get stuck in a jar again. Well, at least not when you're alone!"

Gooey Louie laughed. "Oh, that might be hard, but I'll try," he said.

As they were about to leave the basement, they heard another strange noise coming from behind a stack of boxes. When they moved the boxes aside, they found Fizzwhizz, the small, sparkly monster, trapped under a heavy box.

"Help!" he yelled.

Creeperella and Snickerdoodle rushed over to him and tried to lift the box, but it was too heavy.

CREEPERELLA AND THE NINE MISCHIEVOUS MONSTERS

"We need to get more help," Creeperella said.

She ran upstairs and called for the other monsters. Soon, they were all down in the basement, trying to free Fizzwhizz, except Blunderbuss. After a lot of struggling, they finally managed to lift the box. Fizzwhizz crawled out from underneath, looking a bit shaken.

"Thanks," he said.

"You're welcome," the others replied.

"I'm glad you're okay," Snickerdoodle added.

Fizzwhizz smiled. "I am too," he said. "I thought I was going to be stuck there forever."

CREEPERELLA AND THE NINE MISCHIEVOUS MONSTERS

Just then, they heard a loud crash coming from the kitchen and hurried upstairs. Upon arrival, they found Blunderbuss standing in the middle of a mess. He had knocked over a vase of flowers, and the petals were scattered all over the floor.

"Oh no," Creeperella said.

"I'm so sorry," Blunderbuss apologised. "I didn't mean to."

"It's okay," Creeperella said. "We can clean it up."

The monsters spent the next half-hour cleaning up the mess. When they were finally done, they all sat down in the living room to relax.

"That was a crazy day," Creeperella said.

"It was," Gigglefang agreed.

"But it was crazy fun," Wobblewomp added.

Everyone laughed. It was true. Despite all the chaos, they had all had a great time. As they sat there, talking and laughing, Gooey Louie suddenly jumped up. "Okay, everyone, I have an idea," he said.

The other monsters looked at him curiously.

"What is it?" Creeperella asked.

"Let's have a pillow fight."

The others cheered, grabbed pillows, and started throwing them at each other, filling the room with feathers and laughter. It was a chaotic and messy scene, but it was also a lot of fun. The monsters laughed and played until they were all exhausted. Finally, they collapsed on the floor, panting.

"That was the best pillow fight ever," Gigglefang said.

"I'm so tired," Creeperella groaned.

"Me too," Gooey Louie said.

The monsters all lay there for a while, catching their breath. Then, one by one, they started to fall asleep. It was a funny and peaceful end to a chaotic day.

5: GIGGLES' GREAT GOBLIN GAMES

"Alright, everyone, gather 'round!" Giggles the Goblin announced, his voice echoing through the cavern like a mischievous melody. He was the same small, green goblin with a laugh so big it could fill the entire cavern. Giggles was always up for a good time, and today was no exception.

"Right now, we're going to play a new game," he suggested, his eyes sparkling with excitement like a thousand tiny fireworks. "It's called 'Monster Madness.'"

The other monsters groaned in unison, their collective sigh reverberating off the cavern walls. They had heard of this game before, and it wasn't exactly their favourite. But Giggles was nothing if not persistent, and he wasn't the kind of monster you say no to.

"Oh, come on, it'll be fun," he insisted, his grin widening to an almost impossible degree. "We'll divide into teams, and then we'll have to complete a series of challenges. The first team to finish wins!"

The monsters reluctantly agreed, knowing that resistance was futile when it came to Giggles and his boundless enthusiasm. Giggles quickly divided them into two teams.

"Team Creeperella," he announced, pointing to Creeperella, Wobblewomp, and Blunderbuss. "And Team Gigglefang," he continued, pointing to Gigglefang, Snickerdoodle, and Zippityzap.

The first challenge was to find a hidden treasure chest. Gigglefang's team was off to a good start, but then Blunderbuss, in his usual clumsy fashion, tripped over a rock and spilled the treasure chest all over the ground.

"Way to go, Blunderbuss," Creeperella murmured while rolling her eyes as she always does when things didn't go her way.

"Sorry," Blunderbuss said sheepishly, his cheeks turning a shade of pink that clashed horribly with his green skin. In the end, Gigglefang's team managed to find the treasure chest and win the game.

"See, I told you it would be fun," Giggles said, laughing so hard he nearly fell over. The other monsters groaned again, but they couldn't help but smile. Giggles the Goblin was just too much fun to be mad at.

"Alright, let's move on to the next challenge," the Goblin announced, clapping his hands together. "This one is called 'The Obstacle Course.'"

He led the monsters to a series of obstacles that he had set up. There were slippery slopes, swinging vines, and a giant ball pit that looked like it had been borrowed from a particularly chaotic children's play area. The monsters groaned again. This looked like it was going to be tough.

"Don't worry," Giggles said, his eyes twinkling with mischief. "It's not as bad as it looks, trust me!"

The first team to go was Team Creeperella. Creeperella went first, and she managed to navigate the obstacles with ease, her long limbs making it look almost effortless. Wobblewomp went next, but he kept bouncing off the walls like a particularly enthusiastic rubber ball. Blunderbuss went last, and true to form, he managed to knock over several of the obstacles, causing a domino effect that left the course in disarray.

Team Gigglefang went next. Gigglefang was a natural at the obstacle course. He flew through the air like a monkey, swinging from vine to vine with ease. Snickerdoodle was also very good, her tiny wings giving her an advantage. But Zippityzap kept getting stuck on the slippery slopes, his electric blue fur sparking with frustration. In the end, Team Gigglefang won the obstacle course.

With a boisterous laugh, Giggles gleefully remarked, "You see, I was right all along! This event is an absolute blast!" He laughed so much that he had to hold his sides to ease the ache. The other monsters groaned again, but they couldn't help but smile. Despite any initial frustration, Giggles' infectious fun and laughter quickly dissolved any feelings of anger.

"Alright, let's move on to the final challenge," the Goblin announced, pulling out a scroll of paper. "This one is called 'The Riddle Challenge.'"

He started to read the riddles, his voice echoing through the hollow.

The first riddle was: "I have a neck but no head, I have a mouth but no tongue. What am I?"

Creeperella raised her hand. "A bottle," she said confidently.

Giggles nodded. "Correct. Next riddle: I have a bed but no sleep, I have a cover but no warmth. What am I?"

Wobblewomp raised his hand. "A river," he said, his voice bubbling with excitement.

Giggles nodded again. "Correct. Next riddle: I have a face but no eyes, I have a mouth but no teeth. What am I?"

Blunderbuss raised his hand. "A clock," he said, his voice full of uncertainty.

Giggles shook his head. "Incorrect. The answer is a mountain."

Blunderbuss looked disappointed, his shoulders slumping.

"Don't worry," Gigglefang said, patting Blunderbuss on the back. "There's still time for us to catch up."

The next few riddles were more difficult, but eventually, Team Gigglefang managed to answer them all correctly.

"We did it!" Gigglefang shouted, his voice echoing through the cavern.

"We won!" Snickerdoodle cheered, her tiny wings flapping with excitement.

Giggles laughed, his voice filling the cavern. "Congratulations," he said. "You're the winners of Monster Madness."

The groans of the other monsters filled the air, but their smiles betrayed their true feelings.

"Now, let's celebrate," Giggles said. "I've got a surprise for you all."

He led the monsters to a nearby hidden cave. Inside, there was a giant table filled with food. There were sandwiches, cookies, and even a giant cake that looked like it had been made by a particularly enthusiastic baker. The monsters, full of enthusiasm, let out cheers of delight as they began to dig into their food, their laughter echoing off the walls of the cavern. They ate until they were full, then they sat around the campfire and told stories, their voices mingling with the crackling of the fire. The day had been filled with nothing but perfection, and as the monsters prepared for sleep, a smile of pure joy graced each of their faces. Giggles the Goblin had once again brought fun and laughter to their lives, and they couldn't wait to see what he would come up with next.

6: SNEEZY THE SNIFFLER

"Hmm... I think I smell something wickedly delicious," Sneezy said, sniffing the air. He was the tiny, pink creature with a long, floppy nose and an incredible sense of smell.

"That's probably Giggles cooking again," Creeperella said, indicating her familiarity with Giggles' culinary disasters.

"I bet he's burning something," Wobblewomp added.

Sneezy followed his nose to the kitchen, where he found Giggles standing over an enormous stove, stirring a pot of something that looked suspiciously like mud.

"What is that?" Sneezy asked, wrinkling his nose.

"It's my secret recipe," Giggles replied proudly. "Monster's Stew."

Sneezy took a deep breath and closed his eyes. "It smells... interesting," he said cautiously.

"You'll love it, I promise," Giggles insisted.

Sneezy took a small spoonful and tasted it. His face scrunched up in complete disgust.

"That's awful!" he said.

Giggles just laughed. "You're just not used to my cooking yet. Wait until I have it fully cooked."

Sneezy wasn't sure if he wanted to argue. He decided to just eat his own lunch, which was a much more appetising bowl of berries and honey.

CREEPERELLA AND THE NINE MISCHIEVOUS MONSTERS

After lunch, Sneezy decided to go for a walk. As he wandered through the forest, sniffing the air and enjoying the fresh breeze, he heard a strange noise coming from a nearby clearing. He followed the noise and stumbled upon a group of tiny, furry creatures playing hide-and-seek. They were all different colours and shapes, and they were making a lot of noise. Sneezy watched them for a while, amused. He had never seen creatures like these before. Suddenly, one of the creatures spotted Sneezy. It let out a squeak and ran away. The other creatures followed. Sneezy laughed. "I'm not going to hurt you," he called after them. The creatures stopped and looked back at him. They seemed hesitant, but they didn't run away. Sneezy took a step closer. "Can I play with you?" he asked. The creatures exchanged glances. Then, one of them nodded. Sneezy smiled. He joined the creatures in their game. He was a lot smaller than them, but he was very fast and agile. He managed to hide in some very clever places, and he was always the last one to be found. The creatures were in awe of Sneezy's skills. They had never met a monster like him before. But after a while, the creatures started to tire. They all sat down in a circle and started to tell stories. Sneezy listened intently. He had never heard stories like these before. They were full of surprise and adventure. But soon, Sneezy knew it was time to go. He waved goodbye to the creatures and continued on his walk. As he was walking, he heard a rustling in the bushes. He stopped and looked around. Suddenly, a small, brown creature jumped out of the bushes. It was a squirrel.

"Hello there," Sneezy said.

The squirrel chirped and scampered up a tree.

Sneezy laughed. "You're a quick one, aren't you?" he said.

He continued on his walk, feeling happy and content. He had had a wonderful day. As he was walking back to the monster cave, Sneezy heard another strange noise coming from behind a tree. He stopped and listened. The noise sounded a little different, it sounded like someone crying. Sneezy crept closer to the tree and saw a small blue creature sitting on the ground, sobbing.

"Are you okay?"

The creature looked up at him with tear-filled eyes.

"My toy," it whimpered. "I lost my toy."

Sneezy felt sorry for the creature. He knelt down and gently patted it on the head.

"Don't worry," he said. "We'll find your toy."

Sneezy started searching the area, sniffing the air. He followed his nose to a nearby stream. There, he found the creature's toy. It was a small, stuffed animal. Sneezy gave it back to the creature. The creature's face lit up with joy.

"Thank you so much," it said.

"You're welcome."

He watched as the creature hugged its toy tightly. Then he turned and continued on his walk, feeling a sense of peace and contentment. He had helped a creature in need, and that made him feel really good. When he arrived back at the cave, he found the other monsters gathered around the campfire.

"Where have you been?" Creeperella asked.

"I was just taking a walk."

"Did you find anything interesting?" Gigglefang asked.

"Yes. I met some new friends."

He told the other monsters about the creatures he had met in the forest. They were amazed. They had never heard of creatures like those before.

"They sound like they would be a lot of fun to play with," Wobblewomp said.

"Maybe we should go and visit them sometime," Creeperella suggested.

Sneezy smiled. "That would be great," he said.

As they sat around the campfire, listening to Sneezy's stories, the other monsters couldn't help but feel they now had something else to look forward to.

7: Fizzy AND NIBBLES

"I'M BORED," FIZZY THE Fizzler whined, bouncing up and down on his pogo stick. Flipping energetically was Fizzy's way of expressing his dissatisfaction at not finding something fun to do. He was a bubbly, yellow creature with a fizzy personality and always full of spare energy.

"Why don't you go outside and play?" suggested Creeperella.

"There's no one to play with," Fizzy pouted.

"If so, you could chase after those floating dandelion seed pouches," Creeperella suggested.

"It's too sunny," Fizzy pouted.

"How about we have a water balloon fight?" Gigglefang asked.

Fizzy's eyes lit up. "Deadly! That sounds like fun!"

The monsters grabbed their water balloons and headed outside. They spent the next hour laughing and splashing each other until they were all soaked to the bone.

"I'm worn-out," Fizzy said, flopping down on the grass.

"Me too," Creeperella agreed.

They all lay there in the sun, drying off. It was a rare peaceful moment, and for a while, they all just enjoyed the silence. Then, Gigglefang started laughing.

"Remember that time I accidentally turned Blunderbuss into a giant blueberry?"

The others found that very funny, their laughter echoing through the muted forest. It was a good day.

After a while, Fizzy sat up and looked around. "I'm hungry, guys."

"Me too," Creeperella agreed.

They all went back inside and made themselves sandwiches. As they were eating, Fizzy started to think about his life.

"I'm so lucky to have such great friends," he said.

"I share the same sentiment," Creeperella responded.

"I'm glad we're all here together," Gigglefang added.

After they finished eating, Fizzy decided to go for a walk. He wandered through the forest, enjoying the fresh air. As he was walking, he came across a stream and found a group of tiny, colourful fish swimming in the water.

Fizzy smiled. "Hello there," he said.

The fish looked at him curiously. Then, one of them swam closer.

"What's your name?" Fizzy asked.

The fish bubbled up a few bubbles. "Fizz," it said.

Fizzy laughed. "That's a funny name," he said. "My name is Fizzy too."

The fish swam around Fizzy, nibbling at his toes. Fizzy tickled them, and they giggled. Fizzy spent the next while playing with the fish, loving their bubbly personalities and bright colours. When it was time to go, Fizzy said goodbye to the fish. They waved to him as he swam away.

When he returned, Creeperella wanted to know what he had been up to.

"Where have you been?"

"I went for a walk, and I made new friends by the river."

"Really? What kind?" they enquired.

He told the other monsters about the fish he had met in the stream.

"They sound like they would be a lot of fun to play with," Wobblewomp said. "Perhaps we could go down there to have fun with them next time."

Fizzy smiled. "I'm sure they would love that. They're great fun."

Then there was also Nibbles the Nibbler. "Is there a bite anywhere in this house? I'm starving, and does anyone care?" Nibbles the Nibbler whined, rubbing his stomach and showing off his sharp teeth as he was always on the lookout for his next meal. But this time, he wasn't alone in feeling this way. Creeperella was the first to respond, and she did so in a tone that sounded a little impatient because she was becoming weary of the constant moans of the other monsters.

"I know, I know. We'll eat soon."

"But I'm really starving! My hunger is such that I could eat a thousand slugs neat." Nibbles insisted.

"Well, a thousand slugs might not do you; maybe you should try eating something those rocks over there," Wobblewomp suggested.

Nibbles chuckled. "Sounds like you missed the memo."

"Memo? What memo?"

"Because you asked, I might as well let you in on a well-kept secret. Astonishingly, rocks are actually regarded as delicacies, because they taste so yummy...! However, I would like to eat something else today."

Then he started rummaging through the kitchen cabinets, looking for something to eat.

"Nibbles, stop that!" Creeperella scolded. "You're going to break something."

Nibbles just ignored her. He pulled out a jar of pickles and started munching on them before washing them down with the vinegar left in the jar.

"Those are mine," Creeperella protested.

"Oh, come on," Nibbles said, stuffing the last pickle he was holding into his mouth. "It's just a pickle."

"Well, that was my pickle!" Creeperella sighed, knowing she was fighting a losing battle. "I swear, Nibbles, you're going to eat yourself out of this house one day."

"Maybe I should just start eating the house," Nibbles replied.

CREEPERELLA AND THE NINE MISCHIEVOUS MONSTERS

Creeperella shook her head. "You're hopeless; I don't even know why I waste my time with you."

Just then, Gigglefang burst into the kitchen, laughing. "Guess what, guys? I found a secret passage in the basement."

Nibbles' eyes lit up. "Can we go explore it?"

"Sure," Gigglefang said. "But don't eat anything you find."

Nibbles nodded. "I promise."

The three of them went downstairs to the basement. They found the secret passage behind a loose brick. It was dark and narrow, but it led to a hidden room. Inside the room, there was a treasure chest. Gigglefang opened it and found a pile of gold coins.

"Wow!" Nibbles exclaimed. "Look at all that gold!"

Gigglefang smiled. "We can use this to buy food."

Nibbles' eyes lit up. "Can we buy lots of food?"

"Yes, as much as you want."

Nibbles was so excited that he started to jump all over the floor.

"We're rich!" he shouted.

"Don't get too excited like that," Creeperella said. "We still have to get out of here."

Gigglefang nodded. "Let's go," he said.

They left the basement and headed back upstairs. As they were walking, Nibbles started to think about all the food he was going to eat.

"I can't wait to sink my teeth into a giant pizza," he said.

"Me too," Gigglefang replied.

CREEPERELLA AND THE NINE MISCHIEVOUS MONSTERS

"And, don't forget; lots of ice cream," Nibbles added. "And I mean, lots of ice cream."

Creeperella laughed. "You're going to get sick," she said.

Nibbles just shrugged. "It's worth it, isn't it?" he said.

When they got back to the kitchen, they found the other monsters waiting for them.

"What took you so long?" Wobblewomp asked.

"We found a secret passage," Gigglefang said.

"And we found a treasure chest," Nibbles added.

The other monsters were amazed. They couldn't believe that Gigglefang had found a secret passage.

"Can we see the treasure?" Fizzy asked.

Gigglefang nodded and pulled out the gold coins.

The other monsters' eyes widened. They had never seen so much gold before.

"Wow," Creeperella said. "We're rich."

"We can buy anything we want; all the monster fun stuff," Nibbles said, his eyes sparkling.

The other monsters laughed. They knew that Nibbles was going to eat his way through all the money they earned.

"We should celebrate," Gigglefang said. "Let's have a feast."

The other monsters agreed. They spent the next few hours cooking food and setting up the table. When the table was finally set, they all sat down and started to eat; but Nibbles ate so much that he could barely move.

"I'm stuffed," he said, patting his stomach.

The other monsters laughed. They were all full, too. Afterwards, they played games and shared stories. It was a perfect day. As they were getting ready for bed, Nibbles looked at the treasure chest.

"I wonder what we should do with all this."

"We could buy a new house," Creeperella suggested.

"Or we could donate some to charity," Wobblewomp added.

"Or we could just keep it. We are monsters, remember? We're not humanitarians; so leave charity to humans and other creatures like that and let monsters be monsters, for goodness' sake," Gigglefang said.

Nibbles thought about it for a while. Then, he smiled.

"Calm down, everyone and listen to me. I exactly know what we should do," he said.

The other monsters looked at him curiously.

"I agree with Gigglefang; let's keep the gold, all of it. In fact, we should have another party; a bigger one this time. Let's blow all this gold!"

The other monsters agreed and cheered. They couldn't wait for the next party. As they went to sleep, Nibbles dreamed of mountains of food and endless amounts of gold. He couldn't wait for the next day to come.

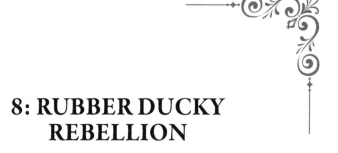

8: RUBBER DUCKY REBELLION

The next morning, Squishy woke up feeling a bit groggy and a whole lot more paranoid. He scanned his room, expecting to see the rubber ducky lurking ominously in a corner. But it was nowhere to be found. Shrugging off the unease, he clambered out of bed, determined to forget about the whole ordeal. But as he shuffled towards the kitchen for breakfast, a peculiar sound emanated from the bathroom. It sounded like... tiny footsteps. Squishy's heart raced. He tiptoed to the bathroom door and peeked inside.

There, in the bathtub, sat the rubber ducky, surrounded by a miniature army of even smaller rubber duckies. They were brandishing tiny, rubber weapons and chanting, "Down with Squishy! Down with the bath!"

Squishy's eyes widened in disbelief. The rubber duckies were revolting! And they were planning to overthrow him! He quickly retreated to his room and grabbed his trusty pillow. Armed with his fluffy weapon, he marched back to the bathroom and confronted the rubber ducky army.

"Stop this madness!" he bellowed, waving his pillow around like a madman. "You can't overthrow me!"

The rubber duckies remained unfazed. They charged at Squishy, their tiny pitchforks raised high. Squishy swung his pillow, toppling several of the duckies. But there were too many. He was quickly overwhelmed. Just as all hope seemed lost, Squishy heard a familiar voice.

"Squishy! What's going on?"

It was Creeperella. She had heard the ruckus and come to investigate. She stormed into the bathroom and scattered the rubber ducky army with a single wave of her hand.

"What were you doing to my duckies?" she demanded, glaring at Squishy.

CREEPERELLA AND THE NINE MISCHIEVOUS MONSTERS

Squishy recounted the entire ordeal, from the rubber ducky's eerie smile to its attempted coup. Creeperella listened patiently, her expression growing more and more amused.

"Well, I suppose that's one way to start your day," she said, finally. "But next time, maybe try a more peaceful approach. Perhaps offer them some chocolate pudding or something."

Squishy nodded. He knew she was right. He had learned a valuable lesson that day: even the smallest of creatures can harbour grand ambitions. And sometimes, the best way to deal with a problem is to offer a bribe.

The incident with the rubber ducky army left Squishy feeling a bit shaken. He had never imagined that something as seemingly harmless as a bath toy could pose such a threat to his well-being. But he also realised that he couldn't let the fear of the rubber duckies control his life.

So, he decided to confront his fear head-on. He went back to the bathroom and picked up the rubber ducky that had started the whole mess. He examined it closely, trying to find something unusual about it. As he scrutinised the ducky, he noticed a small, almost invisible mark on its underside. It resembled a tiny symbol, almost like a hieroglyph. Squishy couldn't decipher its meaning, but he had a hunch that it was somehow linked to the ducky's strange behaviour.

He decided to show the mark to Creeperella. She examined it for a moment, then shook her head. "I've never seen anything like it before," she said. "But it definitely looks ancient."

Squishy wondered if the mark might be some kind of computer code. He had heard stories about coded Groccolli objects that could be dangerous if not handled properly. Could the rubber ducky be one of those objects?

As Squishy pondered this, he began to feel a strange sensation. It was as if something was pulling at him, drawing him towards the bathtub like a magnet. He resisted the urge to go, but it was too strong. He found himself walking towards the bathtub, almost in a trance.

When he reached the bathtub, he saw that the rubber ducky was glowing with a faint, neon light. The symbol on its underside was pulsing, as if it were alive. Squishy hesitated for a moment, then reached out and touched the ducky. As soon as his fingers made contact, he felt a surge of energy flow through him. It was like a wave of electricity coursing through his body, filling him with a sense of power.

Then he heard a voice. It was the voice of the rubber ducky. "You have activated me. Now, you must help me."

Squishy was baffled. What did the rubber ducky want him to do?

"There is a darkness coming; a darkness that will consume this world. You must stop it!"

Squishy felt a sense of dread. He didn't know what the darkness was, but he knew that he had to do something to stop it. He looked at the rubber ducky, and for the first time, he saw it not as a threat, but as a friendly Groccolli.

"I'll help you," he said. "Whatever it takes."

And so, Squishy and the rubber ducky embarked on a quest to save the world from digital darkness. It was a journey filled with danger, adventure, and a whole lot of rubber ducky-related shenanigans. But in the end, Squishy and his unlikely ally proved that even the smallest of creatures can make a big difference.

9: Twinkle's Twirling Triumph

Twinkle the Twirler was a creature of pure energy. Her pink fur sparkled like a disco ball, and her laughter was utterly infectious. But there was one thing Twinkle adored above all else: spinning. She'd spin until she was dizzy, her world a whirling blur of colour and motion. It was her way of expressing herself, her way of letting loose. However, there was a little problem. Gigglefang, the grouchy green monster, just couldn't stand her. He was all about order and quiet, and Twinkle's spinning was the antithesis of both.

"Twinkle, stop spinning!" he'd yell, his voice a high-pitched squeak. But Twinkle would just giggle and spin faster.

One day, Gigglefang had had enough. He decided to put a stop to Twinkle's twirling once and for all. So, how does he plan to do that? Well, he concocted a wicked plan; actually, a devilish scheme that would teach Twinkle an unforgettable lesson. He enlisted the help of Creeperella, the creepy, crawly monster, and Wobblewomp, the wobbly, waddling monster. Together, they set a trap and waited until Twinkle was spinning particularly fast, her world a kaleidoscope of colours. Then, Gigglefang lunged, grabbing her from behind. Creeperella and Wobblewomp joined in, holding Twinkle down. She struggled and kicked, but they were too strong.

"Let me go!" she screamed, her voice a panicked yelp.

"Not until you promise to stop spinning," Gigglefang said, his eyes glinting with malice.

Twinkle was terrified. She'd never been held down before. She felt like a trapped bird, struggling to escape. She knew she had to do something, but what?

Then, a thought occurred to her. She remembered a secret passage she'd discovered under the couch. If she could wriggle free, she could crawl through the passage and escape.

DANDY AHURUONYE

CREEPERELLA AND THE NINE MISCHIEVOUS MONSTERS

With a burst of her last strength, Twinkle broke free from Gigglefang's grip. She scrambled towards the couch and burrowed underneath. The passage was dark and narrow, but she squeezed through. When she emerged on the other side, she found herself in an unfamiliar room filled with shelves of books and scrolls, and there was a large, glowing crystal in the centre of the room. Twinkle had never seen anything like it.

Just as she was about to explore her new surroundings, she heard a noise. It was Gigglefang, Creeperella, and Wobblewomp, searching for her. They were calling out her name, their voices growing louder. Twinkle knew she had to hide. She quickly ducked behind a bookshelf and held her breath. The monsters passed by, their footsteps echoing throughout the room. When they were gone, Twinkle emerged from her hiding place. She decided to explore the rest of the room. Afterwards, she picked up a book and began to read. It was a story about a brave little monster who overcame great challenges. Twinkle was inspired. She realised that she didn't have to let Gigglefang and his friends control her. She could be brave, just like the monster in the book.

With newfound determination, Twinkle made her way back to the main room. She knew that Gigglefang and his friends would be waiting for her, but she wasn't afraid. She had a plan. She waited until the monsters were distracted. Then she crept up behind them and tackled them to the ground. The monsters were caught off guard. They struggled and kicked, but Twinkle was too quick for them.

"You're never going to stop me from spinning!" she declared, her voice filled with triumph.

Gigglefang, Creeperella, and Wobblewomp were defeated. They realised that they couldn't stop the twirler from twirling. From that day on, they left her alone to spin to her heart's content. And Twinkle, the Twirler, was happier than ever.

But Gigglefang, being the stubborn creature he was, couldn't let go of his grudge against her. He spent weeks plotting his revenge, devising a new plan that was even more sinister than his last. He enlisted the help of a new ally, a slimy, slithering monster named Slitherfang. United in purpose, they conspired to create a mechanism—a spinning wheel—that would ensnare Twinkle and oblige her to spin indefinitely, without ever finding a moment of rest.

Slitherfang, with his knowledge of ancient craft, created the spinning wheel. It was a gigantic wooden contraption with a large, circular platform that rotated at incredible speeds. A marvellous barrier that prevented anyone from entering or leaving surrounded the platform. When the spinning wheel was complete, Gigglefang and Slitherfang lured Twinkle to a secluded area of the forest. They pretended to be lost and asked Twinkle for help. Twinkle, being the kind-hearted creature she was, agreed to help them.

As Twinkle approached the spinning wheel, she felt a strange sense of unease. Something about the wheel seemed off. But before she could react, Gigglefang and Slitherfang pushed her onto the platform. The platform began to rotate, faster and faster. Twinkle found herself trapped. She tried to grab onto the sides of the platform, but they were too slippery. Despite her screams for help, the wind drowned out her voice.

As the spinning wheel continued to rotate, Twinkle felt herself becoming dizzy and nauseous. She closed her eyes, trying to focus on something else. Then she remembered the book she had read in the secret room; the story about the brave little monster who overcame great challenges. Twinkle realised that she had to be brave. She had to find a way to stop the spinning wheel. She looked around for anything that could help her. It was then that she spotted a small wooden lever on the side of the wheel. With a surge of adrenaline, she reached out and pulled the lever.

The spinning wheel slowed down, then stopped. Twinkle was free.

CREEPERELLA AND THE NINE MISCHIEVOUS MONSTERS

Shock washed over Gigglefang and Slitherfang. They had never seen anything like it. Twinkle had somehow managed to stop the spinning wheel. Twinkle turned to face Gigglefang and Slitherfang.

"You're never going to stop me from spinning," she declared, her voice filled with triumph.

Gigglefang and Slitherfang realised that they were defeated. They had tried everything they could to stop Twinkle, but nothing had worked. They knew that they could never change Twinkle's love for spinning. From that day on, everyone left Twinkle alone, and Twinkle, the Twirler, was free to spin to her heart's content, knowing that no one would ever stop her again.

10: A Grumbler's Day

"A day so bright, a sky so blue, And yet, Grumble's mood is through."

Grumble, the grumpy grey gremlin, was having a day that would make a tornado seem like a gentle breeze. He was slumped on the couch, his frown so deep, it could've swallowed a small rodent, muttering about everything being "terrible."

"What's the matter with you today, Grumble?" Creeperella asked, her voice dripping with concern. She was wearing her Groccolli wings that morning.

"Everything," Grumble replied, his voice a thundercloud. "The weather's too sunny, the food's too bland, everybody around me is too noisy, and my slippers are too fluffy."

Gigglefang, a lanky monster with a laugh that could shatter glass, tried to lighten the mood. "Hey, maybe you should go for a walk," he suggested. "Get some fresh air."

Grumble groaned. "Walking? That's even worse. It's too tiring, and the pavement's too hot."

Creeperella sighed. "Grumble, you're being ridiculous. It's a beautiful day."

Grumble scoffed. "Beautiful? Pa! More like another conspiracy to make me even more miserable."

Just then, a strange, high-pitched noise echoed through the room. It was a sound Grumble had never heard before. He looked around, his eyes wide with confusion.

"What was that?" he asked.

Gigglefang shrugged. "Don't look at me; I don't know. Maybe it's a new monster or something."

Grumble stood up and walked towards the window. The noise was coming from outside. He peered out and saw a tiny winged creature hovering above the garden. It was bright green and had large, sparkling eyes.

"Ah, I see; It's a Groccolli!" Creeperella exclaimed.

Grumble narrowed his eyes. "A Groccolli? That's ridiculous. Groccollis don't exist."

However, as the Groccolli approached, Grumble came to the realisation that it was undeniably authentic. And, to make things even more interesting, it was heading straight for him. The Groccolli landed on Grumble's shoulder and looked up at him with its big, innocent eyes. Grumble tried to swat it away, but the Groccolli was too quick; trying to swat a Groccolli was always a futile effort due to their remarkable agility.

It flitted around his head, giggling and twirling. After trying a few more time to catch the little robot monster, Grumble gave up trying to catch it but its presence still irritated him.

"Stop it!" Grumble yelled. "Go away and leave me alone!"
But the Groccolli just laughed and continued to tease him.
"I won't leave you alone until you cheer up a little," it told him.
Grumble was starting to get angry. e reached out and grabbed the Groccolli, holding it tightly in his fist.
"Let go of me!" the tiny monster squeaked.
Grumble squeezed harder. The Groccolli squirmed and wriggled, but it couldn't escape. Grumble held on until the Groccolli finally stopped moving. He slowly unfurled his fingers and peered down at the fragile creature lying motionless in his palm. The tiny Groccolli, its delicate wings folded neatly against its body, showed no signs of life. A pang of regret shot through Grumble as he realised that his anger had led to this tragic outcome. He felt a heavy weight of guilt settle in his chest as he acknowledged the consequences of his impulsive actions. With a heavy heart, he gently placed the Groccolli in a small, shallow grave in the garden. As he stood there, the gravity of his actions weighed heavily on him, and he found himself lost in a whirlwind of remorse and self-pity. It was in that moment of solitude that he had a profound realisation - he needed to make a change. He couldn't continue to let his sour mood and selfishness dictate his actions and harm others.

"I'm sorry," he said to Creeperella, Gigglefang, and the rest of the monsters. "I was mean to you."

Creeperella smiled. "It's okay, Grumble. We know you didn't mean it."

Gigglefang nodded. "We all have bad days."

Grumble sighed. "I guess you're right."

He looked out the window at the setting sun. It was a beautiful sight. Grumble realised that there was still a lot of good in the world. He just needed to learn to appreciate it. As the days turned into weeks, Grumble began to make a conscious effort to be more positive. He started taking walks in the park, reading books, and spending time with his friends. He even tried to find humour in everyday situations. The next day, while walking through the woods, Grumble stumbled upon a small clearing. In the centre of the clearing was a tiny, sparkling pond. As he approached the pond, he heard a soft rustling sound. He looked down and saw a small green frog sitting on a lily pad. The frog hopped onto a nearby rock and looked up at Grumble with its big, bulging eyes. Grumble smiled. The monster remembered the late Groccolli he had accidentally killed. He knew that he couldn't bring it back, but he could try to make amends. He reached into his pocket and pulled out a small, colourful flower he had picked on his walk. He tossed the flower into the pond, where it floated gently on the surface.

"This is for you," he said to the frog. "I'm sorry about what happened."

The frog croaked softly as if it understood. Grumble smiled and turned to leave. As he walked away, he looked back at the pond. The flower was still floating on the surface, and the frog was watching it intently. Grumble felt a sense of peace wash over him. He knew that he had a long way to go, but he was starting to make progress. He wasn't the grumpy, miserable guy he used to be. He was starting to enjoy the good things in life and finding happiness in the simple stuff, but what was coming next would really shake him up.

CREEPERELLA AND THE NINE MISCHIEVOUS MONSTERS

The Groccolli's Resurrection

As Grumble sat on the couch the next day, still wallowing in self-pity, he did not realise that something extraordinary was happening in the garden. Beneath the freshly turned earth, a faint glow began to emanate from the tiny grave. Slowly but surely, the Groccolli's wings started to twitch, and then her entire body was enveloped in a shimmering light. Creeperella who was gardening nearby heard the strange rustling sound coming from the spot where they had buried the Groccolli. And as she cleared the grass, she was astonished to see the tiny creature resting there, alive and well. The Groccolli had dug itself out of the grave and was now looking around the garden with a mischievous grin. As Creeperella stood there shocked at what was happening before her eyes, suddenly, she leapt with a joyous cry.

"I'm back!"

Creeperella gasped in astonishment.

The little monster flitted her wings, shaking off the dirt.

"Miss me?" she giggled, hovering in the air.

Creeperella rushed to her.

"Groccolli, how did you...?" She trailed off, awestruck.

Groccolli winked. "Takes more than a grumpy gremlin to keep me down."

Creeperella raised her voice to announce to the other monsters that Groccolli was back as both of them entered the house to meet the monsters, their entrance caused massive chaos as some of them cared that the tiny Groccolli might actually be a spirit or some other bad sign. Gigglefang was upstairs and shouted in a loud voice that echoed through the house as he heard the commotion.

"What's going on here?"

Creeperella called back, "You won't believe it! But by the stars, Groccolli's back!"

Grumble, too, hearing this from the couch, couldn't believe his ears. He hurried to get up his eyes wide with disbelief. There she was,

CREEPERELLA AND THE NINE MISCHIEVOUS MONSTERS

the Groccolli, buzzing about as if nothing had happened. The tiny monster flew right up to him.

"Hey, Grumble. Missed you."

"Groccolli? You're alive!" Grumble whispered, tears welling up in his eyes.

The Groccolli nodded. "I'm a tough little bugger, aren't I?"

Grumble couldn't resist picking up the monster and holding it in his hand. Then, he fell to his knees, a mixture of joy and guilt washing over him. "I'm really sorry for what I did to you," he said. "I was being a terrible monster; so sorry, Groccolli. I didn't mean to—"

Groccolli interrupted him, placing a tiny paw on his nose. "It's okay, Grumble. I'm here now. Let's not dwell on the past."

Gigglefang chimed in, "Yeah, Grumble, it's not every day you get a second chance. Make the most of it, dude!"

Grumble stood up, wiping his eyes. "You're right. I've been a grump for too long. It's time I started appreciating life and all of you."

Creeperella nodded. "That's the spirit, Grumble. We're all in this together."

The monsters spent the rest of the day celebrating Groccolli's return. They laughed, danced, and shared stories, filling the air with joy and camaraderie. As the days went by, Grumble found himself slowly changing. He started to notice the small, beautiful things around him—a butterfly's flutter, the warmth of the sun, the sound of laughter. He realised that life's little joys were always there; he just had to open his heart to them. One evening, as the monsters gathered around for their nightly chat, Groccolli perched on Grumble's shoulder.

"You know," it said, "life's too short to be grumpy all the time. You've got to find the fun in the little things."

Grumble smiled. "You're right, Groccolli. Thanks for showing me that."

Creeperella clapped her hands. "To Groccolli, our little miracle, and to Grumble, our new ray of sunshine!"

Gigglefang and the others joined in the applause. As they all laughed and cheered, Grumble felt something he hadn't felt in a long time—happiness. He realised that, with his friends by his side, every day could be a good day, even for a GGG (grumpy grey gremlin) like him, and besides, the Groccolli's resilience amazed grumble. He realised that even in the darkest of times, there's always hope. And sometimes, the smallest creatures can teach us the biggest lessons. From that day on, Grumble and the Groccolli became inseparable. The Groccolli would follow Grumble everywhere, cheering him up with its laughter and its infectious optimism. And Grumble, in turn, learned to appreciate the little things in life. He realised that being grumpy all the time was a waste of energy and that there was so much more to life than complaining.

Grumble's transformation proved to be a pivotal moment for the entire monster community of Monsterland. His newfound positivity inspired the other monsters to follow suit, gradually turning the once gloomy and miserable monster world into a place filled with fun and joy. All of this was made possible by a tiny Groccolli that had managed to dig itself out of the grave and into Grumble's heart.

11: Monster Mash Mayhem

"A motley crew, a quirky band, In a city hidden, a secret land." The Monster Mash, as they were fondly referred to, was a group known for their chaotic nature. They weren't your typical fearsome monsters. Instead, they were a colourful assortment of beings who loved nothing more than a good prank, a hearty laugh, and a dash of chaos.

Creeperella, the green girl who could vanish into thin air faster than an entertainer's rabbit, was the resident prankster. Gigglefang, a small creature with teeth that could rival a shark's, was the resident comedian. Wobblewomp, a gelatinous blob that changed colour with his mood, was the resident bouncy ball. And Snickerdoodle, a tiny, winged creature with a mischievous twinkle in his eye, was the resident troublemaker.

Blunderbuss, a clumsy giant with a heart of gold, was the resident klutz. Zippityzap was the resident speedster, a lightning-fast creature with electric blue fur. Mumblegrumble, a perpetually grumpy monster with a love for puzzles, was the resident puzzlehead. Tiddlywink was the resident daredevil, a tiny, colourful monster with a big personality. Fizzlebop was the resident optimist, a bubbly monster made of fizzy soda. And Whimsywhirl, a whimsical creature who could create mini whirlwinds with a flick of his wrist, was the resident dreamer.

Today, the Monster Mash had a plan. A big, daring plan. They were going to pull off the biggest prank in the history of Monsterland. Their target? The city's most uptight and grumpy mayor, Mr Grumpington.

"He's gonna flip his lid when he sees this," Creeperella cackled, adjusting her invisible cloak.

"I can't wait to see his face," Gigglefang agreed, his laugh echoing through the sewers.

Their plan was simple, yet brilliant. They were going to turn the entire city upside down. Literally. Using Whimsywhirl's whirlwind powers, they were going to create a giant twister that would lift everything off the ground. Buildings, cars, and even people would be swirling around in the sky.

As the day dawned, the Monster Mash gathered in the heart of the city. Whimsywhirl stood in the centre, his arms outstretched, ready to unleash his whirlwind.

"On three," he shouted. "One... two... three!"

With a mighty roar, Whimsywhirl spun around, creating a massive twister that sucked everything up into the sky. Cars flew through the air, buildings tilted on their sides, and people clung to anything they could find. Mayor Grumpington, who was already in a foul mood, stepped out of his grand mansion only to be caught off guard as a powerful twister suddenly struck. The force of the wind lifted him into the air, sending his briefcase and magnifying glass flying alongside him. As he whirled helplessly, he could do nothing but gaze around in utter shock and disbelief.

"What on earth is happening?" he spluttered.

Meanwhile, the Monster Mash was having a blast. They were flying through the air, laughing and cheering. Creeperella was doing somersaults, Gigglefang was juggling lampposts, and Wobblewomp was bouncing off buildings. The chaos continued for what felt like hours. Finally, Whimsywhirl lost his grip on the twister, and it dissipated. Everything fell back to the ground with a thud. The city was in a state of disarray. Cars were overturned, buildings were damaged, and people were covered in dust. But despite the chaos, there was a strange sense of joy in the air.

Mayor Grumpington, who had landed in a pile of garbage, was furious. He vowed to find the culprits and have them punished. But as he looked around at the smiling faces of the citizens, he realised that, for once, the city wasn't so grumpy; everybody had enjoyed the twister fun.

As it turned out, the Monster Mash had succeeded in their mission. They had turned the city upside down, and they had made everyone laugh. And that, in their opinion, was the best prank of all.

BOOK TWO

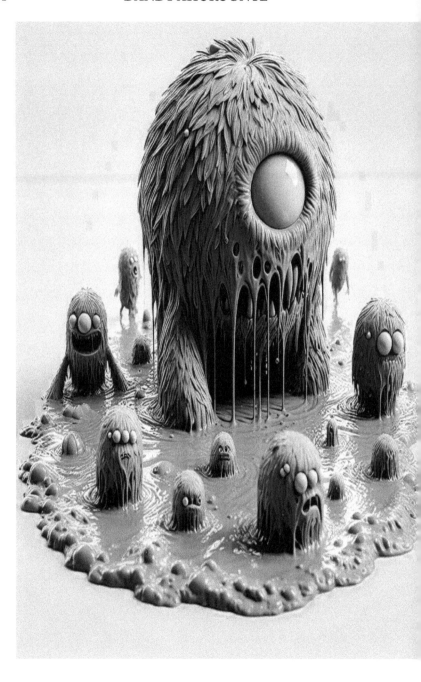

12: The Groccolli MONSTER

"A GROCCOLLI'S LIFE is a bubble, a fleeting thing of joy and fun, a puff of air that pops and disappears." So began the tale of Snizzle, the most mischievous Groccolli in all of Groccolliland. Snizzle wasn't your average Groccolli monster. While most of his kind were content with scaring humans, Snizzle preferred a more... bubbly approach. He loved nothing more than to sneak up on unsuspecting victims, pop a bubble in their face, and watch their startled expressions. One day, Snizzle was on the prowl for his next victim when he spotted a particularly shiny object. It was a golden locket, dangling from the neck of a young girl. Snizzle's eyes lit up. He'd never seen anything so sparkly in his life! He crept closer, his heart pounding with excitement. Just as he was about to snatch the locket, the girl turned around and caught him red-handed.

"You little thief!" she exclaimed; her voice filled with indignation. "What do you think you're doing?"

Snizzle was caught off guard. He stammered and stuttered, trying to explain himself. But the girl wasn't having any of it. She grabbed Snizzle by the tail and tossed him into a nearby pond. Snizzle spluttered and flailed as he tried to swim to the surface. He was a terrible swimmer, and he quickly realised he was in serious trouble. Just as he was about to give up hope, a friendly-looking otter swam up to him.

"Don't worry, I'll help you."

The otter gently nudged him towards the shore, where he was able to climb out of the pond. Snizzle was soaked to the bone, but he was grateful to be alive. He thanked the otter and made his way back to Groccolliland. As he walked through the forest, Snizzle couldn't help but think about the locket. He had wanted it so badly, but now he realised it wasn't worth getting into trouble. He decided that from then on, he would focus on making people laugh instead of trying to steal their belongings. Snizzle's new philosophy quickly caught on among the other Groccollis. They began to see that there was more to life than scaring people. They realised that they could also bring joy and happiness into the world. From that day forward, Snizzle and his friends became known as the "Bubble-Blowing Groccollis." They were no longer feared monsters, but beloved companions who brought joy and laughter wherever they went.

Snizzle's story is a reminder that even the most mischievous creatures can change. It's also a testament to the power of friendship and the importance of finding your own unique way to make a difference in the world.

WARBBLE THE WOBBLY Wonder

"Warbble, the wobbly wonder, a creature of pure glee, Whose dance moves are legendary, a sight to see."

So began the tale of Warbble, a monster unlike any other we've seen so far. He was a walking, talking, dancing dynamo—a total party animal. Unlike those grumpy, scary monsters you see in movies, Warbble was all about good vibes and good times.

Warbble's days were a constant whirl of motion. He'd wake up, stretch his long, lanky limbs, and immediately start swaying from side to side. His body, a vibrant green, seemed to shimmer with energy. His purple hair, a tuft atop his head, bobbed and weaved in time with his movements.

"Morning, everyone!" Warbble would bellow, his voice a cheery rumble. "Let's dance!"

And dance they would. Warbble had a knack for turning any situation into a dance party. He'd break out into a jig during a boring lecture, a waltz in the middle of the market, even a tango during a thunderstorm. His friends loved him for his infectious enthusiasm.

"Warbble's the life of the party," they'd say. "He can turn a frown upside down with just one dance move."

But Warbble's constant movement had its drawbacks. He struggled to sit still, even for the most important occasions. He'd fidget during meals, tap his feet during meetings, and even pace back and forth while trying to sleep.

One day, Warbble's restlessness got the better of him. He was invited to a fancy dinner, and no matter how hard he tried, he couldn't keep his feet still. He wiggled and squirmed, much to the annoyance of the other guests.

"Warbble, please!" whispered his friend, nudging him under the table. "Try to behave just this once."

But Warbble couldn't help himself. He stood up and started dancing right there in the middle of the dining room. The guests were shocked, but the monster didn't

CREEPERELLA AND THE NINE MISCHIEVOUS MONSTERS

care. He was having too much fun and wondered why no one else wanted to enjoy themselves.

"Dance with me!" he shouted, extending a hand to the nearest guest.

To everyone's surprise, the guest actually joined in. Soon, the entire room was filled with dancing monsters, their cheers echoing through the halls.

From that day forward, Warbble was known not just for his energy, but for his ability to bring people together. He proved that even the most unexpected things can be a source of joy, and that sometimes, all you need is a little bit of dancing to brighten up your day.

13: The Flabbergasting Flimflammer

"FIZZGIG, THE FLIMFLAMMER, a fibbing fiend," they'd say, A chatterbox monster, come what may. With a coat of orange, a twinkle in his eye, He'd yap and yabber, till the cows came by. A joker, a storyteller, a master of fun, He'd keep you laughing from morn till night, from sun to sun.

Now, Fizzgig was a chap, a bit of a lad, A fellow who'd jabber, a bit of a gad. He'd tell tales of dragons, of goblins and ghosts, Of treasure and pirates, and all sorts of hosts. But sometimes, his stories, a tad too tall, Would leave his listeners feeling quite small.

One day, at a party, a grand affair, Fizzgig started yapping without a care. He told tales of heroes, of knights so bold, Of battles and dragons, and riches untold. But as he went on, his stories got wilder and wilder, His audience growing ever so milder.

"A dragon," he said, "with scales of gold, And teeth so sharp, they could stories unfold." "A goblin," he said, "with a mischievous grin, Who'd steal your socks, and then hide them within." The crowd laughed and cheered, their eyes wide with glee, But little did they know, the truth was free.

For Fizzgig, you see, was a master of lies, A weaver of tales beneath the skies. He'd spin a yarn, so intricate and fine, You'd swear it was true, divine and sublime. But deep down inside, he knew it was wrong, To deceive his friends with a silly old song.

One day, a wise old owl, with a knowing stare, Said to Fizzgig, "My friend, beware." "Your tales are so grand, so full of delight, But they're not always true, as day and night." Fizzgig thought for a while, his conscience stirred, And realised he'd gone too far; he'd been absurd.

From that day on, Fizzgig, the flimflammer, Began to tell tales that were much calmer. He'd still tell stories of goblins and glimmers, But he'd add a touch of truth to the shimmers. And though he still loved to yap and to chat, He learned to listen, a little bit more than that.

Still, Fizzgig, being Fizzgig, couldn't resist the temptation to embellish his tales just a bit. He'd add a few extra details, a dash of drama, a pinch of humour. And while he might not have been entirely truthful, his stories were always entertaining, always full of life.

Once, a young dragon named Ignis came to visit Fizzgig. Ignis was a bit shy and didn't have many friends. Fizzgig, ever the entertainer, took Ignis under his wing and told him the most incredible stories. He told Ignis about a brave knight who fought a giant, a mischievous goblin who stole a princess's crown, and a wise old wizard who knew the secret to eternal youth.

Fizzgig's tales captivated Ignis. He laughed, he cried, he felt excitement and fear. And most importantly, he felt a sense of belonging. For the first time in his life, Ignis had a friend who made him feel special and accepted.

Fizzgig, seeing the joy he had brought to Ignis, realised that his storytelling wasn't just about entertaining himself. It was about connecting with others, sharing experiences, and making the world a more interesting place. And so, he continued to tell his tales, always striving to balance the truth with the imagination, the real with the fantastic.

And that, my friend, is the tale of Fizzgig, the Flabbergasting Flimflammer; a monster who may have stretched the truth a bit, but whose stories brought joy and laughter to all who heard them.

ZOODLE, THE PURPLE Monster
"A purple blob, a curious sight, With antennae long and tail so tight."

Zoodle, the purple monster, wasn't your average fearsome beast. No, Zoodle was more like a walking question mark, always sticking his nose where it didn't belong. His curiosity was as boundless as the universe, and his tail curled as tightly as a spring.

One sunny morning, Zoodle was wandering through the Misty Mountains, his antennae twitching with excitement. He'd heard rumours of a hidden treasure, a golden Groccolli that was said to grant wishes. Zoodle, being the curious creature he was, couldn't resist the allure of such a prize.

As he ventured deeper into the mountains, the path grew narrower and the air colder. The trees seemed to whisper secrets to each other, and the wind howled like a mega monster. Zoodle shivered, not from the cold, but from the thrill of the unknown.

Suddenly, he heard a faint tinkling sound. It was coming from a small cave hidden behind a curtain of vines. Zoodle crept closer, his heart pounding in his chest. Peering inside, he saw a glint of gold. It was the Groccolli! With trembling hands, Zoodle reached in and grabbed it.

As he pulled it out, it activated and caused a blinding light to fill the cave. When the light faded, Zoodle found himself standing in a lush, green meadow. The mountains had vanished, replaced by a sparkling lake and a gentle breeze.

"Wow," Zoodle exclaimed, his eyes wide with wonder. "Oh, my vinegar, this is deadly awesome!"

He looked around, taking in the beauty of his surroundings. Then, he remembered the Groccolli robot monster. He held it up to the light and made a wish: "I wish I could fly."

Instantly, Zoodle felt a tingling sensation in his body as the machine began to vibrate. He looked down and saw that his feet had turned into wings! With a whoop, he leaped into the air and soared through the sky, feeling the wind rush past him.

Zoodle flew for hours, exploring the new world he had found. He saw other Groccolli creatures, visited captivating forests, and even met a friendly dragon who taught him how to breathe fire. The dragon, whose name was Dragee, was a wise and ancient creature who had lived in the mountains for centuries. Dragee told Zoodle stories of the old days, when the mountains were filled with dragons and every kind of Groccolli.

After a while, Zoodle decided it was time to return home. He flew back to the Misty Mountains and found the cave where he had discovered the little machine. With a heavy heart, he placed the Groccolli back on its pedestal and said goodbye to the magical world he had visited.

As he walked back through the mountains, Zoodle couldn't help but smile. His adventure had been incredible, and he knew he would never forget it. He had made a new friend, learned new skills, and seen things he never thought possible, but most importantly, he had realised his wish to fly.

Zoodle continued his life, always seeking out new adventures and never losing his sense of wonder. And so, the tale of Zoodle, the curious purple monster, lives on—a testament to the power of curiosity and the wonders that can be found in the most unexpected places.

CREEPERELLA AND THE NINE MISCHIEVOUS MONSTERS

14: Grumble the Grumbler

"A BELLY FULL OF FOOD, a heart full of glee, And a mind full of mischief, that's a monster's way."

Unlike most monsters, Grumble the Grumbler didn't fit the mould of your average creature. Sure, he had the usual monstrous features – big green eyes, sharp teeth, and a scaly hide – but his true passion was food. He loved to cook, he loved to eat, and he really loved to talk about food. Now, Grumble wasn't just any foodie; he was a culinary genius who could whip up a feast that would make Gordon Ramsay weep with envy. From his signature "Grumble's Gooey Garlic Gobble" to his "Slimy Spaghetti Surprise," every dish was a masterpiece. But with great culinary skills comes a great appetite. Grumble's legendary appetite left a lasting impression on those who heard about it. For example, he could polish off a whole roast monster, a bucket of bugs, and a vat of slime in one sitting. This often led to a bit of a predicament. When Grumble ate too much, he'd turn into a massive, sleepy lump. And trying to move Grumble when he was in this state was like trying to push a mountain. Consequently, Grumble wasted no time in deciding to host a grand feast for monsters. He invited all his friends—a slimy slug monster named Slippy, a fiery dragon named Flame, and a grumpy goblin named Grog—to come and sample his latest creations. As the monsters dug into their plates, Grumble beamed with pride. He'd outdone himself.

But then disaster struck. As Grumble was enjoying his own feast, he heard a loud crash. Slippy had knocked over a vat of toxic goo, and it was spreading rapidly. The monsters scrambled to escape, but Grumble was too full to move. He was trapped.

Just as it seemed all hope was lost, a tiny, furry creature appeared. It was a brave little mouse named Squeak. Squeak had heard the commotion and had come to investigate. Seeing Grumble's predicament, Squeak knew he had to help. With a determined squeak, Squeak began to nibble away at the toxic goo. It was slow going, but eventually, he managed to clear a path for Grumble. As Grumble stumbled to his

CREEPERELLA AND THE NINE MISCHIEVOUS MONSTERS

feet, he couldn't help but laugh. The bravest little creature in the land had saved him; how fascinating! From that day on, Grumble and Squeak were the best of friends. And whenever Grumble had a bit too much to eat, Squeak was always there to help him out.

But Grumble's adventures didn't stop there. On another day, while exploring the nearby forest, he stumbled upon a hidden cave. Inside, he found a treasure trove of ancient cooking utensils and ingredients. Grumble was ecstatic. He'd never seen anything like it before. With his new-found treasures, the monster chef began to experiment with even more exotic dishes. He created the "Dragon's Breath Curry," a meal so spicy it could melt steel, and a "Goblin's Gold Goulash" so rich it could make a king weep. Grumble's reputation as a culinary genius spread far and wide. Monsters from all over the land came to taste his foods. Even the fearsome King Gruff, known for his picky palate, was impressed. But not everyone was happy about Grumble's success. The evil wizard Goze, who had been trying to take over the kingdom, was jealous of Grumble's popularity and so devised a wicked plot to sabotage Grumble's next feast. Goze slipped a powerful sleeping potion into Grumble's food. When Grumble ate it, he fell into a deep sleep. Goze then took advantage of the situation. He stole Grumble's secret recipe book and tried to use it to create his own powerful potions. But Goze's plan backfired. The potions were so powerful that they caused a massive explosion, destroying his laboratory. Goze was banished from the kingdom, and Grumble was hailed as a hero.

Grumble continued to cook delicious food, make new friends, and have adventures. And whenever he felt like he'd eaten too much, he knew Squeak was always there to help him out.

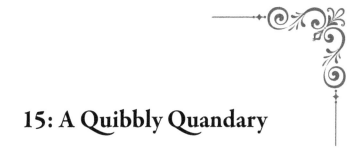

15: A Quibbly Quandary

"QUIBBLY, THE QUIBBLER, a real pain in the little toe, Always arguing and nitpicking, a total farce."

Quibbly was a bit of a know-it-all, a real smart-aleck, if you ask me. He loved nothing more than a good debate, a heated argument, or a friendly competition. And let me tell you, he was really good at it. His intelligence and quick thinking made him a formidable opponent, and he'd argue about anything - the weather, the price of tea and tea's nephew, even the number of toes on a cat. But his argumentative nature could be a bit of a drag, to say the least. It was like living with a walking dictionary, always ready to correct you, nitpick, and find fault. I mean, who needs a friend who's always trying to prove they're smarter than you? Quibbly was a small, spiky monster with a bright yellow body. He had sharp, pointy teeth and a pair of glasses perched on his nose, which made him look a bit like a nerdy hedgehog. And let's not forget his signature quibbling. He'd quibble about the rules of a game, the ingredients in a recipe, even the meaning of a sneeze. It was like having a built-in critic.

That was why everybody worried when Quibbly decided to challenge his friends to a spelling bee. He was sure he'd win. After all, he'd spent hours poring over dictionaries, memorising words, decoding the meaning behind every kind of sneeze, and practising his pronunciation. But to his surprise, he found himself neck and neck with his friend, Squishy, who was a total klutz when it came to spelling.

As the competition heated up, Quibbly started to get a bit nervous. He knew he had to win, or he'd never hear the end of it from Squishy. So, he decided to try a little trick. He whispered a word to Squishy, hoping she'd misspell it. But Squishy, being the good sport that she was, refused to cheat. In the end, Squishy won the spelling bee by a narrow margin. Quibbly was furious. He couldn't believe he'd lost to a total klutz. But as he stormed off, he couldn't help but feel a twinge of admiration for Squishy. She'd played fair, even when it meant losing. And that's when Quibbly realised that maybe, just maybe, there was more to life than arguing and winning. Maybe it was okay to lose sometimes, especially if it meant keeping your friends. This made him change and become less argumentative and more open-minded. He even started to enjoy spending time with his friends without feeling the need to prove himself. And while he never completely lost his love for a good debate, he learned to appreciate the value of compromise and respect.

One day, Quibbly was sitting on a hilltop, watching the sunset. He thought about how much he'd changed since the spelling bee. He realised that sometimes, the most valuable lessons come from the most unexpected places. And in the end, it was Squishy, the klutz who couldn't spell, who had taught him the most important lesson of all: that it's okay to be wrong, and that it's even more important to be kind.

A Clumsy Monster's Mishaps

"A monster might stumble, but a heart can't fumble." So some monsters say. And Krumble, well, he was a living, breathing example of that. He deviated from the usual terrifying monster archetype. No, Krumble was more like a giant, fluffy teddy bear who'd had one too many bowls of bug and worm soup. You see, Krumble had a knack for tripping over his own feet. It was like his legs had a mind of their own, and they were determined to have a little dance party whenever they could. He'd step out of bed in the morning and nearly faceplanted on the floor. He'd try to walk across a room and end up tangled in a pile of laundry that wasn't even in the way. Even his own shadow seemed to conspire against him, tripping him up at the most inconvenient moments. Despite his clumsiness, Krumble was a sweetheart. He had a heart as big as a castle and a smile that could light up a gloomy crocodile in labour pangs. He was always there for his friends, offering a helping hand or a kind word. And even though he often made a mess of things, he'd always manage to clean it up with a hearty laugh. But that was until one day when Krumble was out exploring the forest and stumbled upon a tiny, lost Groccolli. The Groccolli was crying her eyes out, and Krumble felt a pang of sympathy. He knelt down and gently asked what was wrong.

"My wings! They're broken; I can't fly back home now."

Krumble's heart went out to the little creature. He knew he wasn't exactly the best at fixing things, but he was determined to help. He carefully picked up the Groccolli and carried her back to his cave. There, he used a leaf as a splint to mend her wings. As the Groccolli's wings healed, Krumble and the Groccolli became fast friends. The Groccolli, whose name was Twinkle, would tell Krumble stories of her make-believe kingdom, while Krumble would regale her with tales of his clumsy adventures.

One day, Twinkle asked Krumble if he'd ever wanted to fly. Krumble laughed and said, "I'd love to, but I'm too clumsy."

Twinkle smiled. "Don't worry, Krumble. I can teach you. Even though I'm a monster, I'm also a Groccolli supercomputer that can make any wish or desire come true."

Twinkle began by assessing Krumble's current abilities.

"Right, let's start with some basics here. Your first challenge is to start flapping those arms of yours. Think of it as trying to shake off a particularly stubborn piece of broccoli stuck between your teeth."

Krumble flailed his arms awkwardly, looking like a windmill gone haywire. Twinkle couldn't help but chuckle.

"Close enough. Now, let's talk about the physics of flight." She explained the principles in a way even Krumble could understand. "It's all about lift, thrust, and a bit of control. Picture coding algorithms in your head. We need to optimise your flapping speed. Once that's done, we'll get started on your flight training. But before all of that, we must do first things first; we need to get you into a harness. This will keep you safe and secure while you learn to fly."

Krumble looked at the contraption with a mixture of trepidation and amusement. It was a bit like a backpack, only with straps that went around his arms and legs.

"I don't know about this, Twinkle," he mumbled, looking a bit sheepish.

"Trust me, Krumble," Twinkle assured him. "It's the only way we're going to get you airborne." With a sigh, the monster allowed her to strap him into the harness. Once he was secure, she stepped back and took a moment to assess her pupil. "Okay, now, let's imagine you're a bird. You flap your wings to lift off the ground." Krumble tried to picture himself as a bird, but it was difficult. He was a monster, after all, not a feathered creature. Nevertheless, he tried to mimic Twinkle's movements, flapping his arms as best he could. "That's it, Krumble!" Twinkle cheered. "You're doing great! Now, let's try to get some height." She asked him to get on a large stone outside the cave. Krumble then took a deep breath and flapped his arms harder. Slowly, he began to rise off the rock; it was about a foot from the ground. He felt a surge of excitement as he floated a few inches above the cave floor.

"Look at you, Krumble!" Twinkle exclaimed. "You're flying!"

Krumble grinned from ear to ear. He was doing it! He was actually flying! But then, just as quickly as he had risen, he started to descend. He flapped his arms frantically, but it was no use. He was falling! "Don't panic, Krumble! Just relax and let me help you." With a flick of her wings, Twinkle flew over to Krumble and steadied him on the rock again. "Remember, Krumble, you need to keep your balance. If you tilt too far to one side, you'll lose control. I can see that you're halfway there, mate. Now, for the fun part: let's try to get you airborne the way real birds do." With Twinkle's guidance, he continued to practise his flying. He learned how to hover, how to turn, and even how to do a loop-the-loop, albeit a rather wobbly one. Next, Twinkle tapped into her supercomputer brain, crafting a custom code tailored to Krumble's physiology. "I've written a programme that will send signals to your muscles, ensuring you flap with the right rhythm and force. Hold on, this might tickle a bit!" Krumble felt a mild tingling sensation as Twinkle's programme took effect. "Now, let's try again," she instructed. This time, as Krumble flapped, he could feel his body becoming lighter. "I think I'm doing it!" he exclaimed, a hint of triumph in his voice. After several weeks of practical training and computer coding, Krumble was finally ready to take his solo flight. Twinkle watched him with a mixture of pride and excitement as he jumped off from the cave entrance and soared for a moment before landing heavily.

"You did well, Krumble!" she called out. "You're slowly becoming a real flying monster!"

For the final lesson, she positioned Krumble on the edge of a higher cliff and gave him a gentle nudge. "Remember, lift and thrust. And don't forget to enjoy the view while up there because from now going forward, that'll be your new normal!" Krumble launched himself off the edge, flapping his arms with all his might. For a moment, he felt like a boulder plummeting to the ground, but then something amazing happened. Thanks to the Groccolli power, his flapping arms generated enough lift, and he began to soar. Krumble was determined to do better. The next day he practised on his own as he took off once more and soared better, and he kept at it day after day and got better each time, until one day when he took to air and began to fly like a pro. That day, Krumble looked back at Twinkle and gave her a thumbs-up. He was now feeling a free. He was flying. And he had Twinkle, his Groccolli supercomputer friend, to thank for it all. "Look at me,

Twinkle! I'm flying!" he shouted, his voice filled with exhilaration. Twinkle flew beside him, guiding him through the air. "You're doing brilliant, Krumble! Let's try new manoeuvres."

They spent the next days weaving through trees, dodging branches, and performing aerial acrobatics. Krumble's confidence grew with each passing moment. As they landed back in the clearing on that final day, he was breathless but elated.

"I did it! I really did it!"

Twinkle nodded proudly. "You sure did. See what a bit of determination, a supercomputer brain, and some well-timed programming can achieve?"

"Thanks, Twinkle. You're the best friend a clumsy monster could ask for."

Twinkle patted his shoulder. "And you're the best student a Groccolli supercomputer could hope to teach. Now, let's get some rest. Tomorrow, we'll work on long-distant flying, as well as perfecting your landing; it's still a little rough and hard."

Finally, one sunny afternoon, Krumble took to the skies. He soared above the trees, the wind whipping through his fur. For the first time in his life, he felt truly free. And as he looked down at the world below, he couldn't help but smile. He may have been clumsy, but he was also brave, kind, and full of wonder. And that was what truly mattered. From that day forward, he was known as the Flying Monster. And although he still tripped over his own feet from time to time, Krumble never let it get him down. He knew that even the clumsiest monster could make a difference in the world.

Grumble Still Grumbles

"A noodle, a noodle, the bendy old noodle, A twist and a turn; always a flexible joodle."

So began the next tale of Grumble, a monster unlike any other. As already shown, he wasn't your everyday fearsome fiend; no, Grumble was a creature of unadulterated flexibility. He could contort his body

CREEPERELLA AND THE NINE MISCHIEVOUS MONSTERS

into shapes that would make a yoga master weep, and he loved nothing more than a good game of "Twisty the Noodle."

Now, Grumble wasn't exactly the cheeriest chap. His constant bending and twisting had left him a bit more... well, grumpy. Hence the name. But don't let his sour demeanour fool you. Deep down, he was a softie with a heart of gold.

One day, he was out and about, minding his own business while looking to do good to others after the recent events when he stumbled upon a peculiar sight. It was a group of tiny, fluffy creatures called "Fluffins," and they were absolutely terrified of seeing him.

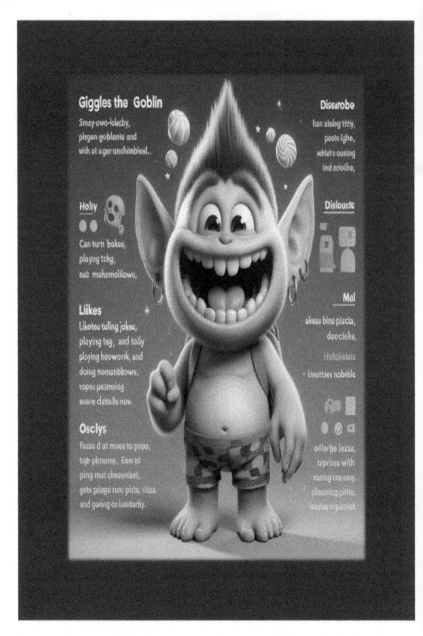

It turned out a wicked monster robot named Hagatha had stolen their precious Fluffin-berries and was threatening to turn them into her personal snack. Of course, he clearly understood why a monster would desire to snack on Fluffin-berries because he too loves to eat; but Grumble, being the good-hearted monster that he was now becoming, couldn't bear to see the Fluffins suffer. So, he decided to take matters into his own hands, or rather, his own noodly body.

With a twist and a turn, he managed to sneak into Hagatha's lair. Inside, the monster robot was cackling away, surrounded by a pile of Fluffin-berries. Grumble crept closer, his heart pounding with a mixture of fear and determination. He knew he had to be quick, but also quiet. With one dramatic twist, he coiled himself around Hagatha, trapping her in a tangle of noodly goodness.

The evil robot squirmed and screamed, but it was no use. Grumble held tight, his grip as firm as a lobster's. The Fluffins cheered from a safe distance, their tiny voices filled with hope.

Finally, Hagatha gave up. She surrendered the Fluffin-berries, and Grumble, with a triumphant wiggle, released her. The Fluffins were overjoyed, and they thanked Grumble wholeheartedly.

However, he was not content to simply save the day. He wanted to make sure that Hagatha would never be able to harm the Fluffins again. So, he decided to teach her a lesson. With a mischievous glint in his eye, he suggested they play a game of "Twisty the Twister."

Hagatha, still reeling from her defeat, reluctantly agreed. Grumble, with his expert twisting skills, quickly gained the upper hand. He twisted and turned her this way and that until she was dizzy and disoriented.

Finally, Hagatha had enough. She begged Grumble to stop, promising never to bother the Fluffins again. Grumble, satisfied, agreed. He released the robot, who stumbled away, looking decidedly less confident.

The Fluffins were incredibly grateful to Grumble for his kindness, bravery, and ingenuity. They celebrated their victory with a feast of Fluffin-berries, and Grumble joined in the festivities.

From that day forward, Grumble was known throughout the land as the hero who saved the Fluffins. He continued his adventures, twisting and turning his way through life, always ready to lend a helping hand to those in need. And though he may have been a bit grumpy at times, there was no denying that Grumble was a truly remarkable monster.

Lessons and principles to be gleaned from this tale:

Bravery and Determination: Facing fears head-on with a mix of courage and resolve can lead to great victories.

Kindness and Compassion: Helping others in need, regardless of their differences, fosters gratitude and strong bonds.

The Importance of Teaching Lessons: Ensuring that wrongdoers understand the impact of their actions can prevent future misdeeds.

Flexibility and Adaptability: Embracing one's unique abilities can lead to innovative solutions and triumphs in challenging situations.

16: A Predicament

"A PUDDLE'S LIFE AIN'T all sunshine and rainbows, ye know," Grumble the Grumbler would often grumble, his voice as deep and rumbling as the thunder that often accompanied his complaints. He was, after all, from the Grumble family, known as masters of the art of grumbling, experts of the whine. Still, this particular Grumble was a peculiar fellow; a water-loving monster who'd rather be splashing about in a puddle than being anywhere else. He had turquoise skin, webbed feet, and a pair of gills that looked like a couple of old, retired fish. He was a bit on the small side, but his grumbles were as big as a whale. Now, Grumble had a problem. A big, wet problem. You see, he'd invited a bunch of his pals over for a water party. It was supposed to be a grand old time experience, with water balloons, water fights, and all sorts of aquatic shenanigans. But then, the heavens opened up, and it started pouring like a leaky bucket. The party was ruined in a classic manner.

"This is a disgrace," Grumble grumbled, his voice echoing through the rain-soaked forest. "A water party on a rainy day? It's like having a fish fry without any fish!"

His friends, a motley crew of water-loving monsters and water-spitting gremlins, tried their best to cheer him up. "Don't worry, Grumble," said a cheerful-looking monster named Splash. "We can still have fun. We can just play in the puddles."

"Puddles?" Grumble scoffed. "Did I just hear you suggest playing in the puddles? That's like eating a biscuit without any jam."

Just then, a mischievous-looking monster named Bubble popped up from the puddle beside Grumble. "Hey, Grumble," he said with excitement. "I've got a better idea. Let's have a puddle jumping contest."

Grumble's eyes lit up. "A puddle jumping contest?" he said. "Now that's an idea worth grumbling about."

And so, the puddle jumping contest began. Grumble, being the grumbler that he always was, was determined to win. He launched himself into the air, his webbed feet propelling him forward. But just as he was about to land, a gust of wind blew him off course. He landed in a particularly deep puddle, soaking himself to the skin.

"Blast!" he grumbled, shaking the water out of his ears. "I'm a soggy mess."

But even though he was wet and still bad-tempered, he couldn't help but smile. After all, a good grumble is always worth a little soak. And as he sat there, surrounded by his friends, enjoying the rain, he realised that maybe life wasn't so bad after all. Even a professional grumbler can have a little fun. As the rain continued to pour, he and his friends continued to play. They splashed and they jumped and they laughed. They even started singing a silly little song about puddles. And as their voices echoed across the forest floor, Grumble knew that he had made the right decision, because even on a rainy day, a puddle of any kind can be a lot of fun. By the time the next day arrived and the sun was shining brightly, the puddles had dried up. Grumble and his friends stood on the edge of the forest, looking out at the sparkling lake. "That was a great day," he said, his voice softened by a smile. "I know now that even a grouch can have a little fun." And so, Grumble the Grumbler continued to live his life, splashing and having a generally good time. And whenever anyone asked him if he was happy, he would simply reply with a memorable one-liner: "As happy as a puddle in the rain."

Monster Griggle's Adventure

"A monster's mirth, a jolly sight, can turn the darkest day to light."

CREEPERELLA AND THE NINE MISCHIEVOUS MONSTERS

Griggle wasn't your average monster. While his family had a well-earned reputation for being a bit on the gloomy side, Griggle was a beacon of brightness. Sure, he had a knack for finding the funny side of even the most mundane situations, but his cheerful disposition was anything but scary. His laughter was like a contagious disease, spreading joy and good cheer wherever he went. However, Griggle's infectious humour often overshadowed his more serious side. People would laugh and laugh at his jokes, but when he tried to say something important, like, say, "Please pass the butter," they'd often burst into giggles. It was a bit frustrating, you might say. Enough was enough. Griggle was determined to prove that he was more than just a walking joke. He wanted to show the world that he had depth, intelligence, and a whole lot of sass. So, he set off on a grand adventure to find the legendary Groccolli Golden Grumble Stone, a Groccolli artefact said to grant its owner the power to make anyone laugh or cry at will. His journey took him through treacherous mountains, across raging rivers, and into the heart of the Groccolli wonder forest. Along the way, he met a variety of colourful Groccolli characters, including a talking squirrel named Nigel, a grumpy troll named Harold, and a mischievous toy named Pip. Nigel, with his sharp wit and quick tongue, was a constant source of amusement for Griggle. Harold, despite his cantankerous exterior, was actually quite lonely and yearned for companionship. And Pip, with her playful pranks and mischievous grin, was always up to something.

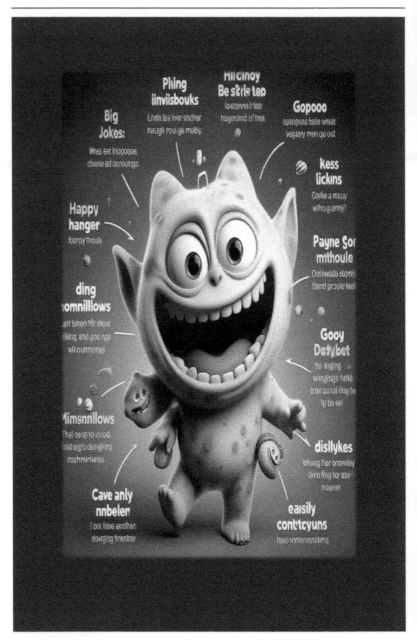

Together, the group faced every kind of challenge and danger. They battled Groccolli beasts, solved tricky puzzles, and outwitted a

CREEPERELLA AND THE NINE MISCHIEVOUS MONSTERS

particularly clever Groccolli enemy. But through it all, Griggle's laughter never faltered. His infectious cheer lifted the spirits of those around him and helped them overcome even the most daunting obstacles.

Finally, after a long and arduous journey, Griggle found the Groccolli Golden Grumble Stone. But as he reached out to grab it, a giant, hairy monster burst out from the ground below and snatched it away. The monster, it turned out, was a fearsome creature known as the Grumble-Snatcher, who had been searching for the stone for centuries. The Grumble-Snatcher was a terrifying beast with razor-sharp teeth and claws. It roared with such ferocity that the ground trembled beneath their feet. Griggle and his friends knew they were in serious trouble.

But they were not about to give up without a fight. Nigel, with his quick thinking, devised a plan. He suggested that they use the Grumble-Snatcher's own fear against him. They would tell him a scary story, so scary that it would frighten him into dropping the Groccolli stone. Harold, despite his grumpiness, was the perfect storyteller. He spun a tale so terrifying that even the bravest of creatures would have shuddered. He described a monstrous creature that lived in the darkest depths of the forest, a creature that could turn even the bravest hearts to stone. As Harold told his story, the Grumble-Snatcher's eyes grew wide with fear. He trembled, and his grip on the Groccolli loosened. With a final, desperate effort, Griggle snatched the stone from the monster's grasp and ran as fast as he could. The dragon chased after them, but he and his friends were too quick for him. They escaped into the nearby forest, where they hid until the monster had given up the chase.

As Griggle held the Groccolli Golden Grumble Stone in his hands, he suddenly realised that he didn't need it to prove himself. His laughter, his kindness, and his infectious cheer were enough. He was more than just a joke machine; he was a friend, a companion, and a source of joy for everyone he met. And so, Griggle returned home a hero, his reputation as a grumbler forever tarnished by his incredible adventure. From that day forward, people no longer laughed at his jokes; they laughed with him and respected him. And Griggle, for the first time in his life, was truly happy.

Lessons learned:

The power of positivity: Griggle's infectious laughter and cheerful disposition helped him overcome challenges and inspire others.

True friendship: The bond between Griggle and his friends showed the importance of loyalty, support, and teamwork.

Overcoming fears: By facing his fears and confronting the Grumble-Snatcher, Griggle proved that courage can triumph over adversity.

The value of individuality: Griggle's unique personality and sense of humour made him a beloved character, demonstrating that it's okay to be different.

BOOK THREE

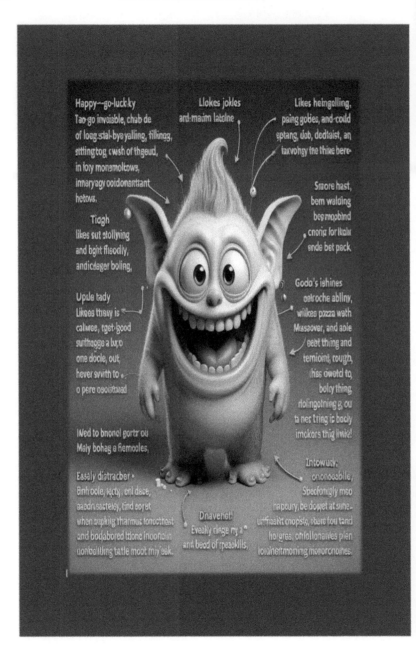

17: Monster Nyaka & The Vet Dilemma

"SOMETIMES, THE QUIRKIEST creatures have the most peculiar preferences," Creeperella mused, a mischievous sparkle in her eyes. She had never said those words before, but now that she had, they perfectly captured the mysterious nature of Monster Nyaka, the newest resident in their monstrous neighbourhood.

Monster Nyaka was peculiar, even by monster standards. She was tall and gangly with fur that changed colour depending on her mood and eyes that seemed to glow with an inner light. But what truly set her apart was her absolute, unwavering hatred for vets. Yes, you heard it right; Nyaka despised vets with an almost comical passion. She would rather face a thousand tickle fights with Gigglefang than set foot in a vet's office.

One day, as Creeperella and her friends were lounging around their favourite cave, Nyaka burst in, her fur a bright, angry red.

"What's got your fur in a twist, Nyaka?" asked Giggles the Goblin, his ever-present grin widening.

"It's those blasted vets!" Nyaka huffed, her eyes blazing. "I can't stand them! They're always poking and prodding and treating me like some sort of science experiment."

Creeperella raised an eyebrow. "Well, you do need to see a vet sometimes, Nyaka. It's important for your health."

Nyaka crossed her arms defiantly. "Not if I can help it. I've decided to choose my own vet and pay for my own treatments. That way, I can make sure I get someone who treats me with the respect I deserve."

The other monsters exchanged amused glances. This was classic Nyaka – always finding a way to do things her own way.

"Alright, Nyaka," Creeperella said, trying to hide her smile. "If that's what you want, then go for it. Just make sure you find a good one."

Nyaka's fur shifted to a more relaxed shade of blue. "Oh, I will. I've already found the perfect vet. She's kind, gentle, and she doesn't treat me like a lab rat."

Gigglefang snickered. "Sounds like you've got it all figured out, Nyaka."

Nyaka nodded proudly. "I do. And I'm willing to pay for it myself. No offence, Creeperella, but I don't trust anyone else to choose my vet."

Creeperella laughed. "None taken, Nyaka. As long as you're happy and healthy, that's all that matters."

And so, Nyaka began her visits to her chosen vet, a kind-hearted monster named Dr Fluffernutter. Everyone knew Dr Fluffernutter for her gentle touch and her ability to make even the most stubborn monsters feel at ease. Nyaka's fur would turn a calm, contented green whenever she returned from a visit, and she would regale the other monsters with tales of her vet adventures.

One day, as they were gathered around their usual spot, Nyaka came in with a big smile on her face.

"You won't believe what happened at the vet today," she said, her eyes sparkling with excitement.

"Oh, do tell," said Snickerdoodle, her tiny wings fluttering with curiosity.

"Well," Nyaka began, "Dr Fluffernutter had this new gadget that she wanted to try out. It's called a Fur-Fluffer, and it makes your fur all soft and shiny. I was a bit sceptical at first, but she convinced me to give it a try."

CREEPERELLA AND THE NINE MISCHIEVOUS MONSTERS

Giggles the Goblin leaned in, his eyes wide with interest. "And? How did it go?"

Nyaka's fur turned a bright, happy yellow. "It was amazing! My fur has never felt so soft. I feel like a brand-new monster!"

The other monsters laughed and cheered, happy to see Nyaka so pleased.

"Sounds like Dr Fluffernutter is worth every penny," Creeperella said with a grin.

"She is," Nyaka agreed. "And I'm so glad I found her. I don't know what I would do without her."

Creeperella couldn't help but feel a sense of pride.

18: Dr Fluffernutter

ONE BRIGHT AND SUNNY morning, Dr Fluffernutter was bustling around her clinic, preparing for a busy day. Her clinic was a cosy little place, filled with colourful decorations and the soothing scent of lavender. As she arranged her tools and gadgets, she hummed a cheerful tune. Just then, the doorbell chimed, and in walked Monster Nyaka, her fur a vibrant shade of green.

"Good morning, Nyaka! How are we feeling today?"

"Morning, doctor, I'm feeling pretty good, but I thought I'd come in for a check-up."

"Excellent idea," Dr Fluffernutter said, adjusting her glasses. "Let's get started, shall we?"

As she settled into the examination chair, Dr Fluffernutter began her usual routine, checking Nyaka's fur, eyes, and ears. She chatted away, telling Nyaka about a new gadget she was working on – the Tickle-Tonic, a special tonic that could make even the grumpiest monsters giggle. Nyaka laughed, her fur turning a happy yellow.

"That sounds amazing, Dr Fluffernutter. I can't wait to try it."

After the check-up, Dr Fluffernutter brought out the Fur-Fluffer, her latest invention. "How about a little fluffing to make your fur extra soft and shiny?"

Nyaka nodded eagerly. "Yes, please!"

As Dr Fluffernutter worked her wonders with the Fur-Fluffer, Nyaka's fur transformed into a silky, shimmering coat. Nyaka beamed with delight, her fur a radiant gold.

"Thank you," Nyaka said, giving the vet a big hug. "You always know how to make me feel better."

Dr Fluffernutter smiled, her eyes twinkling behind her glasses. "It's my pleasure, Nyaka. I'm always here for you."

As Nyaka gracefully exited the sunlit clinic, Dr Fluffernutter meticulously tidied up her workspace, ensuring everything was in perfect order for her next patient. Her commitment to her work was unwavering, and she took great pride in the opportunity to help her patients feel their best. Whether it was a routine check-up to ensure optimal health or the exploration of a groundbreaking new medical invention, Dr Fluffernutter approached every task with boundless enthusiasm, compassion, and an unwavering dedication to providing exceptional care. Throughout the day, she busily prepared for the highly anticipated tea party she was hosting later in the afternoon. Laughter and lively conversations filled the clinic as her friends and patients gathered around the beautifully set table, savouring delectable treats and exchanging heartwarming stories. As the sunset signalled the end of the tea party, Dr Fluffernutter surveyed the scene, her heart filled with a profound sense of fulfilment. She knew that, through her work, she was touching lives and spreading joy, one furry friend and beaming smile at a time.

Early the next day, Dr Fluffernutter bustled around her clinic, preparing for another busy day. Her first patient was Gigglefang, who had come in for his annual check-up.

"Good morning, Dr Fluffernutter!" Gigglefang greeted her with a wide grin. "Ready to make me giggle?"

Dr Fluffernutter chuckled. "Always, Gigglefang. Let's get started so you can giggle all you want."

As she examined Gigglefang, they chatted about his latest pranks and jokes. Gigglefang shared his best joke. It began as soon as he arrived holding a cup of drink which he then placed on the table and waited for an opportunity to spring a wicked joke. It didn't take long before the vet glanced around and saw him sipping from the cup; even though the vet wasn't exactly sure what was in the mug, she was utterly surprised that the monster was having some kind of a drink and wanted to know more.

"Hang on a moment, Gigglefang; is that tea you're drinking?"

"Oh, no, doctor; it is Tea's brother..., he tastes much better!" In response to what he said, Dr Fluffernutter found it so hilarious that she laughed uncontrollably and almost let go of the stethoscope she was holding. And yet, she managed to pull herself together and continues to examine her patient. Once recovered, she made a remark that indicated she understood the joke.

"By Tea's brother, did you mean coffee?"

"You're clever, vet!" he commended her.

"You're in perfect health, Gigglefang," she said afterwards, still giggling. "Just keep spreading that laughter."

Gigglefang beamed. "Will do, Doc!"

Throughout the day, the doctor eagerly tended to a diverse array of patients, each presenting their own unique quirks and requirements. From Nyaka's constantly shifting fur to Wobblewomp's exuberant and buoyant demeanour, she approached each case with meticulous care and boundless creativity. As the afternoon approached, she invited everyone to gather for a bit of light-hearted enjoyment, transforming the clinic into a lively hub brimming with laughter and animated conversation as her friends and patients congregated around the same communal table. They revelled in delectable treats while regaling one another with captivating tales. Gigglefang, as expected, assumed the role of the merrymaker, regaling the group with comical anecdotes

CREEPERELLA AND THE NINE MISCHIEVOUS MONSTERS

and jests. With a mischievous glint in his eye, he posed a fascinating question.

"Why don't monsters eat ghosts?"

"Why?" all the other monsters chorused.

"Because they taste like vinegar!"

Gigglefang's reply sent everyone into fits of laughter. Afterwards, the vet looked around at her friends with a deep sense of satisfaction;

knowing she was making a difference in their lives, one happy smile at a time.

Profile & Characteristics:

Appearance: Dr Fluffernutter is a small, fluffy monster with fur as soft as a cloud and a pastel pink hue. She has large, round glasses that sit precariously on her tiny nose, and her ears are adorned with colourful, mismatched earrings.

Distinctive Features: Her fur is super soft and fluffy, making her look like she's always surrounded by a pink, cotton candy cloud. Plus, her voice is so gentle that it can calm even the most anxious monsters.

Gentle and Kind: Dr Fluffernutter is known for her gentle touch and kind heart. She treats every monster with the utmost care and respect, making them feel comfortable and safe.

Patient and Understanding: She has an infinite amount of patience, which is essential when dealing with stubborn or scared ogres like monster Nyaka. She takes the time to explain procedures and treatments, ensuring her patients feel at ease.

Quirky and Fun: Despite her professional demeanour, Dr Fluffernutter has a playful side. She loves to make her patients laugh and often tells silly jokes or performs tricks to lighten the mood.

Eccentric Fashion Sense: Dr Fluffernutter has a unique sense of style. She loves wearing bright, mismatched clothes and accessories, which often include oversized bows, colourful scarves, and glittery shoes.

Inventive Treatments: She is always coming up with new and innovative treatments for her patients. From the Fur-Fluffer to the Tickle-Tonic, her inventions are as effective as they are whimsical. She enjoys tinkering in her lab, creating new gadgets and treatments to make her patients' lives easier and more comfortable.

Fur-Fluffer: A sleek, shiny machine that makes fur soft and shiny.

Tickle-Tonic: A special tonic that can make even the grumpiest monsters giggle.

Dreamcatcher 3000: A device designed to capture and replay dreams, still a work in progress but full of potential.

Likes:

Helping Others: Dr Fluffernutter finds great joy in helping her patients feel better. She loves seeing the smiles on their faces after a successful treatment.

Tea Parties: The doctor loves hosting tea parties for her friends and patients. Her tea parties are always filled with fun, delicious treats, tea, and, of course, plenty of 'tea's brother.'

Dislikes:

Rudeness: Dr Fluffernutter has little patience for rudeness or disrespect. She believes in treating everyone with kindness and expects the same in return.

Boredom: She thrives on creativity and innovation, so she dislikes anything that feels monotonous or uninspired.

Messiness: Despite her eccentric fashion sense, Dr Fluffernutter likes to keep her clinic tidy. She believes a clean environment is essential for a healthy mind and body.

CREEPERELLA AND THE NINE MISCHIEVOUS MONSTERS

Weaknesses:

Overly Trusting: Dr Fluffernutter tends to see the best in everyone, which can sometimes lead to her being taken advantage of.

Perfectionist: She can be a bit of a perfectionist, often spending extra time on treatments and building new gadgets to ensure they are just right.

Strengths:

Empathy: Her ability to empathise with her patients makes her an excellent vet. She understands their fears and anxieties and knows how to comfort them.

Creativity: Her inventive mind allows her to come up with unique solutions to medical problems, making her treatments both effective and enjoyable.

Calm Demeanour: Her calm and soothing presence helps to put even the most nervous monsters at ease.

Preferred Food:

Bugs and Honeydew Cake Slices: Dr Fluffernutter has a particular fondness for cakes baked with various bugs and honeydew. She often snacks on them during her tea parties, while treating difficult patients, or while working in her lab.

Preferred Jokes:

The vet finds Gigglefang's jokes very amusing. Gigglefang, with his oversized fangs and constant giggle, is the resident comedian of the monster crew. His jokes are legendary, and he has a knack for making everyone laugh, no matter how bad their day has been. Here's one of his best jokes that the vet loves:

Gigglefang: "Why did the monster sit in the corner during the party?"

Creeperella: "I don't know, why?"

Gigglefang: "Because it wanted to be a little 'goblin' up the fun!"

The vet and other monsters erupted into laughter, with Giggles the Goblin nearly falling off his seat. "That's a good one, Gigglefang!" he said, wiping away tears of laughter.

Gigglefang and The Vet

One bright morning, the vet was bustling around her clinic, preparing for a busy day. Now, guess who her first patient was? Well, it was none other than Gigglefang, who had come in for his regular check-up.

"Good morning, doctor!" he greeted with a wide grin. "Ready for my latest giggles?"

Dr Fluffernutter chuckled. "At all times, Gigglefang. Now, shall we get started?"

As she examined Gigglefang, they chatted about her new gadgets and his latest pranks and jokes. As the day went on, she treated a variety of patients, each with their own unique quirks and needs. From Nyaka's ever-changing fur needs to Wobblewomp's bouncy nature, she handled each case with care and creativity.

As Monster Nyaka has turned out to be one of the quirkiest beasts in Monsterland, let us talk a little more about this unusual dragon. It all began one sunny morning. Nyaka woke up with her fur a bright, cheerful yellow. She stretched her long limbs and yawned, ready to start the day. As she stepped out of her cosy cave, she spotted Creeperella and the gang gathered around a campfire.

"Morning, Nyaka!" Creeperella called out, waving.

"Morning, everyone!" Nyaka replied, her fur shifting to a warm orange as she joined her friends.

"Guess what?" Giggles the Goblin said, his eyes twinkling with mischief. "I've got a new game for us to play if you guys are up to it!"

Nyaka's fur turned a curious green. "Oh? What kind of game?"

"It's called 'Monster Mayhem. It's a scavenger hunt with a twist. We have to find items hidden all over the forest, but there are traps and puzzles along the way."

Nyaka's eyes lit up with excitement. "This sounds like my kind of fun. Count me in!"

As the monsters set off on their scavenger hunt, her fur shifted through a rainbow of colours, reflecting her excitement and curiosity. She darted through the trees, her keen eyes spotting hidden items and her quick reflexes helping her avoid the traps. At one point, she found herself face-to-face with a particularly tricky puzzle. It was a series of levers and gears that needed to be arranged in a specific order to unlock a hidden compartment.

"Need a hand?" asked Wobblewomp, bouncing over to avoid her. Nyaka the puzzle. "I think I've got it, but an extra pair of eyes wouldn't hurt."

Together, they worked on the puzzle as they made progress. Finally, with a satisfying click, the compartment opened to reveal a shiny moonberry muffin.

"Jackpot!" Nyaka exclaimed.

Still, the monsters continued their scavenger hunt, each of them finding hidden treasures and solving puzzles. By the time the sun began to set, they were all exhausted but happy. Back at the campfire, Nyaka shared her prize with her friends. As they sat around the fire, Monster Nyaka couldn't help but feel grateful for her friends and the adventures they shared. But as the fire began to die down, a thought crossed her mind. What would their next adventure be? There were still so many mysteries to uncover and challenges to face. Therefore, as she looked around at her friends, Nyaka knew that whatever came next, they would face it together. And with that thought, she settled down to sleep, her fur turning a peaceful blue.

Appearance:

Nyaka is a gangly monster with fur that changes colour based on her mood. Her eyes glow with an inner light, giving her an almost ethereal appearance. She has long, slender limbs and a removable tail that curls up when she's happy but retracts when she's anxious. Her fur can shift through a spectrum of colours, from bright red when she's angry, to a calm blue when she's relaxed. She also has a pair of small, delicate wings that she uses more for show than for flying. The wings, too, are retractable and allow her to hide them when they're not in use.

Quirky Traits:

Nyaka is fiercely independent and has a mind of her own. She doesn't like being told what to do and prefers to make her own decisions, especially when it comes to her health. Despite her independent streak, Nyaka is incredibly loyal to her friends. She would go to great lengths to protect them and ensure their well-being.

Adventurous Spirit:

Nyaka loves exploring new places and trying new things. She's always up for an adventure, whether it's discovering a hidden cave or trying out a new gadget at the vet. Always on the lookout for the next big adventure, Nyaka's most notable quirk is her intense dislike for vets. She has a deep-seated fear of being poked and prodded, which is why she insists on choosing her vet and paying for her own treatments.

Mood Fur:

The colour changes of her fur make her a walking mood ring. This can be both amusing and helpful for her friends, as they can easily tell how she's feeling. Thanks to Dr Fluffernutter's Fur-Fluffer, Nyaka loves having her fur soft and shiny. She takes great pride in her appearance.

Dislikes:

Vets: Nyaka's biggest dislike is going to the vet.

Being Told What to Do: Nyaka values her independence and doesn't like being bossed around.

Boring Routines: She thrives on excitement and adventure, so she dislikes anything that feels monotonous or routine.

Weaknesses:

Stubbornness: Nyaka's independence can sometimes make her stubborn. She doesn't like admitting when she's wrong or asking for help.

Health Risks: Her intense dislike for vets can sometimes lead to her avoiding necessary medical treatments.

Strengths:

Adaptability: Her ability to adapt to new situations and environments makes her a valuable member of the group.

Courage: Nyaka is brave and unafraid to face new challenges head-on.

Preferred Food:

Nyaka really loves hot worm stew, a special treat she found during one of her adventures. These stews are made from special worms that can only be harvested during a full moon.

Nyaka is not just another monster; she is a dynamic, multifaceted character whose colourful personality and adventurous spirit make her a beloved member of her community. Whether she's standing up for her friends, embarking on a new quest, or finding innovative ways to avoid the vet, Nyaka's story is always worth telling.

19: Nyaka's Mysterious Malady

"SOMETIMES, THE MOST peculiar problems require the most extraordinary solutions," Nyaka muttered to herself, her fur a worried shade of purple. It was time for another visit to see the vet specialist, Dr Fluffernutter. Normally, Nyaka would have done anything to avoid this, but today was different. She was feeling terribly ill, and even her usual tricks to dodge the vet couldn't help her now. Her fur was a sickly red, and she felt as if a thousand tiny goblins were doing a jig inside her stomach. "Alright, Nyaka, let's get this over with," she grumbled to herself as she trudged towards Dr Fluffernutter's clinic. As she entered, the familiar scent of lavender and the sight of colourful decorations did little to lift her spirits. The vet greeted her with a warm smile, her fluffy fur looking as soft as ever.

"Good morning, Nyaka! What seems to be the problem today?" she asked, adjusting her oversized glasses. Nyaka plopped down on the examination chair. "That's the problem. I don't know, Dr Fluffernutter. I just feel awful. My stomach hurts, my head is spinning, and my fur won't stop turning red."

Dr Fluffernutter frowned, her brow furrowing in concern. "Hmm, that does sound serious. Let's see what we can do."

She began her usual routine, checking Nyaka's fur, eyes, and ears. But no matter what she did, she couldn't pinpoint the exact cause of Nyaka's illness.

"This is quite the conundrum," the vet said, scratching her head. "I can't seem to figure out what's wrong."

Nyaka sighed with her fur still a frustrated red. "How are you supposed to know how I'm feeling if you can't feel it yourself?"

And then, like a bolt of lightning, an idea struck her. "That's it! I'll build a special diagnosis machine that will let you feel exactly what I'm feeling!"

Dr Fluffernutter's eyes widened in surprise. "That's a brilliant idea, Nyaka! But do you think you can build something like that?"

Nyaka's fur turned a determined blue. "Absolutely. Just give me a little time."

Over the next few days, Nyaka, even though still feeling unwell, worked tirelessly in her cave, gathering parts and pieces from all over the forest.

She tinkered and toiled, her fur shifting through a rainbow of colours as she worked. Finally, after what felt like an eternity, she stood back and admired her creation; the Diagnogram. The diagnosis machine was a pure marvel of monster engineering. It was a sleek, shiny robot with a series of sensors and wires that would allow Dr Fluffernutter to experience Nyaka's symptoms firsthand.

"Alright, let's see if this works," Nyaka said as she lugged the machine to Dr Fluffernutter's clinic. She greeted her with a mixture of curiosity and excitement. "Is this the machine you were talking about?" Nyaka nodded. "Yep! It is called a Diagnogram. All you have to do is wear this headset, and you'll be able to feel exactly what I'm feeling."

Dr Fluffernutter carefully put on the headset, her fluffy pink fur contrasting sharply with the sleek metal of the machine. As soon as she activated it, her eyes widened in surprise.

"Oh, my deadly! This is incredible! I can feel everything you're feeling, Nyaka!" Dr Fluffernutter exclaimed, her voice filled with wonder. Nyaka watched anxiously as Dr Fluffernutter experienced her symptoms. After a few moments, the vet removed the headset and smiled.

"I think I know what's wrong now," she said, her eyes twinkling behind her glasses. "You have a case of the Gremlin Grumbles. It's a rare condition, but fortunately, it's easily treatable."

"Really? That's great news! What do I need to do?"

Dr Fluffernutter handed her a small bottle of Tickle-Tonic. "Just take a spoonful of this every morning for a week, and you'll be back to your old self in no time."

Nyaka took the bottle. "Thank you so much, Dr Fluffernutter. I don't know what I would have done without you."

As Nyaka left the clinic, she felt a wave of relief wash over her. She couldn't wait to tell Creeperella and the others about her adventure.

Back at the cave, her friends, who were eager to hear about her visit to the vet greeted Nyaka.

"So, what happened?" Creeperella asked, her eyes wide with curiosity.

Nyaka grinned. "Well, it turns out I had GG; the Gremlin Grumbles. But thanks to Dr Fluffernutter and my new diagnosis machine, I'm on the road to recovery."

Giggles the Goblin laughed. "Only you, Nyaka, would come up with something as crazy as a diagnosis machine. But I'm glad it worked!"

The monsters gathered around, listening intently as Nyaka recounted her tale. They laughed at her jokes, marvelled at her ingenuity, and cheered when she told them about her recovery. As the monsters settled down for the night, Nyaka couldn't help but feel a sense of pride. She faced a difficult challenge and came out stronger on the other side, and as she drifted off to sleep, she knew more adventures might only be a night's sleep away.

20: MONSTER
Quibblequack

"AN INVENTOR'S MIND is like a monster's playground – full of wild ideas and unexpected surprises," Nyaka often said as she contemplated the essence of her inventive spirit. Monster Nyaka was now known far and wide for her growing list of ingenious inventions. Her cave had become a veritable workshop, filled with gadgets and gizmos that she had created over the years. From replicas of the Fur-Fluffer and the Tickle-Tonic to other gadgets used for everyday activities; Nyaka's inventions were as whimsical as they were practical. Then as Nyaka was tinkering with her latest creation – an improved version of the device her vet called the Dreamcatcher 3000, designed to capture and replay dreams, which Nyaka had now redesigned to make it more powerful – she heard a commotion outside her cave. Curious, she stepped out to see what was going on. To her surprise, she found her friends gathered around a new monster. This monster was unlike any she had ever seen. It was tall, with feathers instead of fur and a beak that looked like it belonged on a duck. Its eyes were a piercing blue, and it had a mischievous glint that made Nyaka's fur stand on end.

"Who is that?" Nyaka asked, her fur turning a curious green.

Creeperella turned to her, a bemused expression on her face. "This is Quibblequack. He's new to the neighbourhood."

CREEPERELLA AND THE NINE MISCHIEVOUS MONSTERS

Quibblequack gave a low bow, his feathers ruffling. "Greetings, everyone. I am Quibblequack, the most unusual monster you'll ever meet."

Nyaka raised an eyebrow. "I'll say. What brings you here, Quibble....qua-qua?"

"Oh, the name is Quibblequack."

"Sorry; excuse my ignorance....! So, I was asking, what brings you to Monsterland, Quibblequack?"

He straightened up, his beak clicking. "I've heard tales of your inventions, Nyaka. I wanted to see them for myself."

Nyaka's fur turned a proud gold. "Well, you've come to the right place; come in let me show you around."

As Nyaka led him into her cave, she couldn't help but feel a little uneasy. There was something about Quibblequack that seemed... a little off. But she pushed the thought aside and focused on showing him some of the inventions she recently collected from her vet.

"This is the Fur-Fluffer," Nyaka said, pointing to a sleek, shiny machine. "It makes your fur soft and shiny."

Quibblequack nodded, his eyes gleaming. "Impressive. What else do you have here?"

Nyaka led him to another corner of the cave. "This is the Tickle-Tonic Mixer. It's an engine used in making the special tonic that can make even the grumpiest of monsters to giggle."

Quibblequack chuckled. "I think I could use some of that."

As they continued the tour, Nyaka showed Quibblequack the latest invention from the vet, the Dreamcatcher 3000. "This device is ultra special; it captures and replays dreams. It's still a work in progress according to what Dr Fluffernutter told me, but I think it has great potential."

Quibblequack's eyes widened. "Fascinating. This is truly genius, Nyaka."

Nyaka's fur turned a bashful pink. "Thank you, Quibblequack. I appreciate that, but all admiration should go to Dr Fluffernutter who is the chief inventor around here."

But as the days went by, it became clear that not everyone was as impressed with Quibblequack as Nyaka was. The other monsters found him strange and a bit too mischievous for their liking. He had a habit of stirring up trouble and causing conflicts among the group. Then one evening, as the monsters gathered around the campfire, Giggles the Goblin voiced his concerns.

"I don't know about this Quibblequack fellow. He's always causing trouble."

Creeperella nodded. "I agree. He's been stirring up arguments and playing pranks that aren't very funny."

Nyaka's fur turned a defensive red. "He's just different, that's all. We should give him a chance."

But the other monsters weren't convinced. They decided to keep a close eye on the visitor, just in case. One day, as Nyaka was servicing the Dreamcatcher 3000, she heard a loud crash outside her cave. She rushed out to find Quibblequack tangled in a mess of wires and gears.

"What happened?"

Quibblequack looked sheepish. "I was trying to fix one of your inventions, but I guess I made things worse."

Nyaka sighed. "Quibblequack, you should have asked for help. My inventions are delicate."

Quibblequack hung his head. "I'm sorry, Nyaka. I just wanted to impress you."

Nyaka's fur softened to a gentle green. "It's alright. Just be more careful next time."

As Nyaka helped Quibblequack untangle himself, she couldn't help but feel a pang of sympathy for him. He was just trying to fit in, after all. But the other monsters weren't so forgiving. They confronted Quibblequack, demanding to know why he was always causing trouble.

CREEPERELLA AND THE NINE MISCHIEVOUS MONSTERS

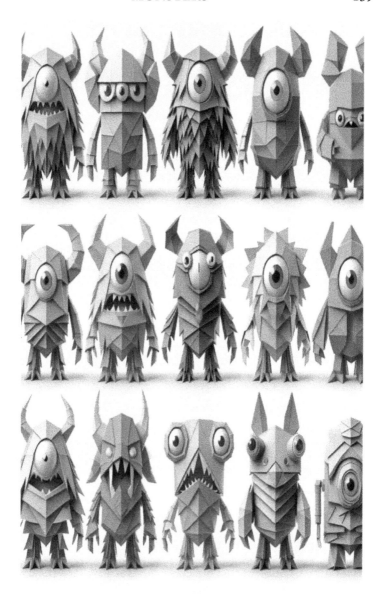

Quibblequack sighed. "I guess I just wanted to be noticed. I've always been different, and it's hard to fit in."

Creeperella's eyes softened. "We understand, Quibblequack. But you need to be more considerate of others."

Quibblequack nodded. "I'll try. I promise."

As the days went by, he made a concerted effort to be more mindful of his actions. He helped Nyaka with her inventions, played fair in their games, and even made an effort to get along with the other monsters. One evening, as they gathered around the campfire, Nyaka shared a new proverb she had come up with.

"A monster's true colours shine brightest in the darkest times."

They nodded in agreement, their eyes reflecting the flickering flames.

Giggles the Goblin grinned. "That's a good one, Nyaka. And I think it applies to all of us."

Quibblequack's Pranks

Quibblequack, with his mischievous glint and playful nature, quickly became known for his pranks. His antics were the talk of the neighbourhood, and while they often caused a bit of chaos, they also brought a lot of amusement. Here are some of his most memorable pranks:

The Feather Frenzy:

Prank: Quibblequack filled Giggles the Goblin's cave with feathers. When Giggles woke up, he was buried under a mountain of fluffy feathers.

Reaction: Giggles emerged from the cave looking like a giant, fluffy bird, much to the amusement of the other monsters. "I guess you could say I had a feather-light sleep!" Giggles joked as he tried shaking off the feathers.

The Invisible Ink Incident:

Prank: Quibblequack replaced the ink in Creeperella's favourite pen with invisible ink. When Creeperella tried to write, nothing appeared on the paper.

Reaction: Creeperella was initially puzzled, but when she realised what had happened, she couldn't help but laugh. "Looks like my thoughts have gone invisible too!" she quipped.

The Slippery Slide:
Prank: Quibblequack coated the entrance to Wobblewomp's cave with a slippery, gelatinous substance. When Wobblewomp tried to leave, he slid right out and landed in a heap.
Reaction: Wobblewomp laughed as he picked himself up. "Well, that was a slippery start to the day!" he said, shaking off the goo.

The Tickle Trap:
Prank: Quibblequack set up a series of tickle traps around the campfire. When the monsters sat down, they were greeted by a flurry of tickles.
Reaction: The monsters erupted into fits of laughter, unable to stop giggling. "Quibblequack, you've really outdone yourself this time!" Nyaka said between giggles.

The Balloon Bonanza:
Prank: Quibblequack filled Blunderbuss's cave with helium balloons. When Blunderbuss entered, the sheer number of balloons lifted him off the ground.
Reaction: Blunderbuss floated around the cave, laughing. "I guess I'm having an uplifting day!"

Nyaka's Proverbs

Nyaka, with her inventive mind and thoughtful nature, often came up with proverbs that reflected her experiences and observations. Here are some of her most memorable sayings:

"Even the quirkiest creatures have a place in the monster world."
Meaning: This saying promotes acceptance and inclusivity, reminding everyone that being different is something to be celebrated.

"A problem shared is a problem halved, but a prank shared is a laugh doubled."
Meaning: This proverb underscores the joy of sharing both challenges and fun moments with friends.

The next day turned out to be a day of mischief and wisdom. That sunny morning, the monsters were gathered around the campfire once more, enjoying a hearty breakfast. With his mischievous reputation preceding him, Quibblequack had a naughty spark in his eye, suggesting that he was planning his next prank.

"What's on your mind, Quibblequack?" Nyaka asked as her fur turned a curious green.

"Oh, nothing much," Quibblequack replied, trying to hide his grin. "Just thinking about how to make today a bit more... interesting."

Giggles the Goblin chuckled. "Uh-oh, that sounds like trouble."

Quibblequack winked. "You'll see."

As the day went on, the monsters went about their usual activities, but they couldn't shake the feeling that something was up. Sure enough, Quibblequack's pranks began to unfold...

MONSTERS OF WOBBLETON

In the whimsical world of Wobbleton, we found another group of ten mischievous monsters different from the earlier ten; they were also causing a delightful ruckus. First, we have Gigglesnort, a furry little creature whose laughter can be heard for miles. He's quite the charmer, with his twinkling eyes and fondness for tickling unsuspecting passersby. However, his weakness is custard tarts; one whiff and he's lost all sense of mischief.

Next up is Bumblethump. With feet too big for his body and a heart just as large, he's always tripping over daisies, which he then lovingly replants. His strength lies in his boundless empathy, but his oversized feet are often his downfall, quite literally.

Then there's Squeebles, a slippery fellow with a love for puzzles. He can wriggle his way out of any tight spot, but if you challenge him to a riddle, he's bound to stick around until he solves it, often forgetting his mischievous plans.

Don't forget about Whifflewharf, the monster with a nose so keen he can smell trouble brewing from ten miles away. His talent for sniffing out secrets is unmatched, but his curiosity often leads him into sticky situations.

Chortlechum is the group's supreme prankster, always ready with a whoopee cushion or a bucket of slime. His joy is infectious, but his pranks sometimes backfire, leaving him in a gooey mess.

In the shadows lurks Monsterella, a shy monster who loves the dark. Her ability to move silently makes her an excellent hider, but her fear of the light means she often misses out on the fun.

Boogleboo is the musical monster of the bunch, with a voice that can cause a landslide. His serenades are legendary, though his inability to carry a tune in a bucket means they're also ear-splitting.

Then there's Muddlefoot, whose muddled thoughts lead to the most unexpected outcomes. His creativity is his strength, but his confusion can make simple tasks hilariously complicated.

Noodleflop is all limbs and no grace, a dancer at heart who can't help but entangle himself in his own moves. His enthusiasm is admirable, but his coordination is not.

Lastly, there's Snickeroo, the sweet-toothed monster who can turn any frown upside down with her confectionery creations. Her baking is her pride, but her insatiable appetite for sweets often leads to a shortage of treats for those gathered with excitement to watch her tricks.

Together, these monsters make Wobbleton a place of endless giggles and japes, where every day is an adventure in laughter and light-hearted mischief. Their antics might be naughty, but their hearts are as golden as the setting sun over Wobbleton's wonky hills. And remember, in Wobbleton, a little bit of mischief is always welcomed with a wink and a smile.

21: The Last Ten Monsters

Bogglewump: Bogglewump is a small, round monster with bright purple fur and three googly eyes. He has tiny wings that are too small for flying but perfect for flapping excitedly; this made other monsters to wonder why he bothered growing wings, anyway. Bogglewump loves hiding behind doors and jumping out to surprise his friends. He giggles uncontrollably when his pranks succeed. There came a day when he decided to prank Snizzle by hiding in a giant pot. But Bogglewump got stuck and couldn't get out! Later, Snizzle came into the kitchen to fetch something and heard a strange noise inside one of the cooking pots and went to investigate; it was then that he saw Bogglewump trying unsuccessfully to free himself from the pot. After the find, he couldn't control himself as he laughed so hard that he too fell over and landed in the same pot. But he was able to free himself and later on the prankster. Bogglewump's favourite food is jellybeans. He loves to mix all the flavours in a big bowl and for reasons unknown to everybody else; he tries eating the beans using a fork instead of a spoon, and he calls it "Jellybean Surprise." He is also a quick thinker, excellent at hiding, and has a contagious laugh; easily distracted by shiny objects.

Bogglewump, the prankster king,
Hides behind doors, ready to spring.
With jellybeans, he loves to munch,
Mixing flavours in a big, fun crunch.

Snizzle: Snizzle is a tall, one-legged monster with green, scaly skin and a long, curly tail. His eyes are always half-closed, giving him a perpetually sleepy look. Snizzle enjoys sneaking up on others and tickling them with his tail. He often falls asleep in the most unusual places. One day, he tried to tickle Wobble, but Wobble's belly was so jiggly that Snizzle ended up tickling himself! They were both in stitches until they couldn't breathe. Snizzle's favourite food is always spaghetti served with slug sauce. He loves to twirl the stuff around his long, curly tail and slurp it up. He calls it: "Tail Twirl Spag." He's stealthy, and has a great sense of humour and climbing things are his strong points, but he's extremely ticklish himself and prone to napping at inconvenient times.

Snizzle sneaks with tail so long,
Tickling friends, he sings a song.
Spaghetti twirls around his tail,
Slurping noodles and lots of slugs.

Flibber: Flibber is a chubby, blue monster with floppy ears and a big, toothy grin. He has a liking for wearing mismatched socks and ignored the laughter and advice of those who tried to advise him against such a practice. Then there was Flibber Joke, one of his favourite pastimes. He once told a joke that was so funny that even Grizzle, the grumpy monster, couldn't help but join in the laugh. I know exactly what you're thinking; you're wondering what Flibber's favourite food might be. Well, it's peanut butter mixed with jelly sandwiches. For him to enjoy it, he loves to make them with extra peanut butter and cut them into funny shapes that make them look so strange, and he calls them "My Funny-face Sambos."

Flibber often gets into trouble for eating things he shouldn't, like crayons, glue, and stuff like that, and he is a great storyteller, has a fantastic sense of taste, and is very friendly. However, he is also clumsy and has a habit of chewing on anything he can get his greasy hands on.

CREEPERELLA AND THE NINE MISCHIEVOUS MONSTERS

Zoodle: Zoodle is a tiny, yellow monster with a long, bendy neck and big, round eyes. He has a tuft of red hair on top of his head. He often got bored and on one of those days, wanted some excitement, and foolishly, Zoodle poked his long nose into a busy beehive, and as expected, he got chased for miles by the bees! What would he do now? Well, he had a great idea; he ran around in circles and zigzags until the bees got tired and left him alone as they all flew away. Phew! That was a narrow escape! But, do you know his favourite food? Wait for it; it is...., Honey! No one loved honey more than Zoodle; oh, how he loved it so much that he drizzled it on everything quite literally, but especially toast. He calls it his HTD, or "Honey Toast Delight."

Zoodle is always curious and loves to explore. He often gets into mischief by poking his nose where it doesn't belong. And his weaknesses are being inquisitive, excellent at finding hidden things, and very flexible, but he's easily scared and tends to get stuck in tight places.

Wobblan: Wobblan is a round, pink monster with short legs and arms. He has a big belly that jiggles when he laughs. You can't help but notice when Wobblan is around; especially at parties or other celebrations. Wobblan's favourite food remains popcorn; his love for both the popping sound and the taste is the reason why he chose to avoid popcorn sold in the shop and often prepares to pop it himself so he can add lots of butter. Not surprisingly, he calls it his "Dancing Popco."

Wobblan dances, belly shakes,
Starts a party, fun he makes.
Popcorn popping, buttered bright,
Dancing monster, pure delight.

Grizzle: Grizzle is furry and grey; a monster with a grumpy expression and a bushy tail. He has sharp claws but a soft heart. Grizzle pretends to be tough but is very kind. Easily annoyed and has a soft spot for cuddles. He enjoys playing board games and often lets others win. The same happened on a games night when he organised a board game and, surprise, surprise, let everyone win, and it turned out to be a successful event and they all had so much fun that they decided to make it a weekly event. Grizzle's favourite food? Ah, pizza! He loves the stuff so much that he often made his own, and of course, with lots of cheese and pepperoni. Guess what he calls it? "Grizzly Pizza Pie."

Puffle: Puffle loves to float around and sprinkle glitter everywhere; making everything around her sparkle but is easily distracted by anything shiny and tends to leave a trail of glitter. She caused a big trouble once. It was after the celebration that the couple realised their mistake; yes, they had foolishly invited Puffle to their wedding. Well, she sprinkled so much glitter that everyone looked like they were covered in stars and went on to have a glitter fight. Puffle's favourite food is cupcakes. She loves to bake them and decorate them with lots of sprinkles. She calls them "My Glittercakes."

Puffle floats and sprinkles glitter,
Makes the world a bit more fitter.
Cupcakes baked with sprinkles bright,
Glitter monster, pure delight.

Mizzle: Mizzle is a small, orange monster with a long, pointy nose and big ears. He has a mischievous twinkle in his eye. Mizzle loves to play tricks and often hides things from his friends. He has a talent for making funny noises. At a soup party one evening, he hid all the spoons, and everyone had to eat their soup with forks! Everybody found it very funny, and, after the dinner, they all chased Mizzle around.

CREEPERELLA AND THE NINE MISCHIEVOUS MONSTERS

Fuzzle: Fuzzle is a round, red monster with short, stubby arms and legs. He has a big, fluffy mane around his neck. Fuzzle loves to hug and often surprises his friends with big, squishy hugs. He enjoys rolling around and playing tag. On a day that Snizzle's eyes were half-closed because he was sleepy, Fuzzle mistook his rather sleepy look for a frown and so went on to hug him; he hugged Snizzle so hard that Snizzle's tail got tangled! They looked at each other and just burst out laughing; afterwards, they spent the rest of the day untangling it. Fuzzle's favourite food is marshmallows, which he loves to roast over a campfire and make s'mores. He calls them his "Fuzzle S'mores."

Fuzzle hugs with squishy might,
Roasts marshmallows in the night.
S'mores so gooey, chocolate bliss,
Fuzzle monster, hugs and kisses.

Doodle: Doodle is a colourful, patchwork monster with a long, wiggly tail and big, expressive eyes. He looks like a living piece of art; he loves to draw and paint, often leaving his artwork everywhere. He enjoys making up stories to go with his drawings. Very artistic, a great storyteller, and very imaginative. Doodle can be messy, though, and tends to get paint everywhere. There was a day when he painted a mural so big that it covered the entire wall of their clubhouse.

22: THE FINALE

"EVERY ENDING IS JUST a new beginning in disguise," Creeperella often said, her vine-like hair swaying gently as she pondered the mysteries of life. This wise saying perfectly encapsulated the wild and wacky world of Creeperella and her nine mischievous monsters.

As we draw the curtains on this fantastical journey, let's take a moment to reflect on the delightful chaos and heartwarming moments that have brought us here. From the giggle-inducing pranks of Giggles the Goblin to the inventive genius of Monster Nyaka, each chapter has been a rollercoaster ride of laughter, mischief, and unexpected surprises.

The Monsters' Greatest Hits

- Giggles the Goblin: The master of pranks, Giggles has kept us in stitches with his feather-filled caves and tickle traps. Remember the time he filled Blunderbuss's cave with helium balloons? "I guess I'm having an uplifting day!" Blunderbuss had joked, floating around like a giant, clumsy balloon.
- Monster Nyaka: With her ever-changing fur and inventive mind, Nyaka has shown us the power of creativity and determination. Her Fur-Fluffer and Dreamcatcher 3000 are just a few examples of her genius. And who could forget her diagnosis machine that helped Dr Fluffernutter feel exactly what Nyaka was feeling? "Sometimes, the quirkiest creatures have the most peculiar preferences," Nyaka had mused, her fur a thoughtful blue.

- Quibblequack: The new kid on the block, Quibblequack has stirred up quite a bit of trouble with his mischievous pranks. But beneath his feathered exterior lies a monster just trying to fit in. His pranks, like replacing Creeperella's pen ink with invisible ink, have left us laughing and shaking our heads. "Well, I guess my thoughts have gone invisible too!" Creeperella had quipped, holding up the blank paper.
- Gooey Louie: The playful blob of blue goo, Louie has bounced and stretched his way into our hearts. His favourite hiding spot under the bed and his love for jellybeans and chocolate pudding have made him a lovable, if slightly messy, friend. Just don't bring out the vacuum cleaner – it's his biggest fear!
- Dr Fluffernutter: The kind-hearted vet with a penchant for inventive treatments, Dr Fluffernutter has been a beacon of comfort and care. Her Fur-Fluffer and Tickle-Tonic have brought smiles to many a monster's face. And her tea parties? Legendary. "Laughter is the best tonic, especially when it's shared with friends," she often said, her eyes twinkling behind her glasses.
- Blunderbuss: The clumsy giant with a heart of gold, Blunderbuss has stumbled his way through many an adventure. His accidental troubles have brought laughter and warmth to the group. "That was a slippery start to the day!" he had laughed, picking himself up after sliding out of his cave.
- Wobblewomp: The gelatinous blob with a bouncy personality, Wobblewomp has danced and bounced his way into our hearts. His love for colourful lights and bouncy castles has made every day an adventure. "A monster's true colours shine brightest in the darkest times," he often said, his fur a vibrant rainbow.
- Gigglefang: The furry creature with oversized fangs and a constant giggle, Gigglefang's jokes have kept us laughing. "Why did the monster sit in the corner during the party? Because it wanted to be a

little 'goblin' up the fun!" he had joked, sending everyone into fits of laughter.

• Snickerdoodle: The tiny, winged trickster, Snickerdoodle's invisibility and love for surprise parties have made her a delightful friend. Her sparkling sugar cubes and mischievous twinkle have brought joy to many a day.

• Zippityzap: The lightning-fast creature with electric blue fur, Zippityzap's energy and agility have made every race an exciting challenge. His love for neon lights and thunderstorms has added a spark to our adventures. "Speed is my middle name!" he often boasted, leaving a trail of sparks in his wake.

• Mumblegrumble: The grumpy-looking monster with a secret love for fun, Mumblegrumble's rhyming when happy and love for puzzles have made him a clever and endearing friend. "Even the quirkiest creatures have a place in the monster world," he often said, his frown turning into a rare smile.

• Tiddlywink: The tiny, colourful adventurer, Tiddlywink's boldness and love for treasure hunts have made every day an exciting quest. Her ability to shrink and grow at will has added a touch of fun to our lives. "A problem shared is a problem halved, but a prank shared is a laugh doubled," she often said, her eyes twinkling with mischief.

• Fizzlebop: The bubbly monster with a body made of fizzy soda, Fizzlebop's cheerful personality and love for bubbles have brought a sparkle to our days. "Life is better with a little fizz," he often said, creating bubbles of all sizes.

• Whimsywhirl: The whimsical creature with a body that swirls like a tornado, Whimsywhirl's dreamy nature and love for daydreaming have added a touch of whimsy to our adventures. "Dreams are the wind beneath our wings," she often said, floating gracefully through the air.

A Final Farewell

As we bid farewell to Creeperella and her nine mischievous monsters, let's remember the laughter, the pranks, and the heartwarming moments that have made this journey so special. Each monster, with their unique quirks and lovable personalities, has taught us the value of friendship, creativity, and a good sense of humour.

So, dear reader, as you close this book, remember that the adventures of Creeperella and her friends are never truly over. "Every ending is just a new beginning in disguise," as Creeperella wisely said. Who knows what new mischief and adventures await them in the future?

The End... Or is it?

What new adventures await Creeperella, Nyaka, Quibblequack, and their mischievous friends? Stay tuned for more delightful tales in the world of Creeperella and her nine mischievous monsters. Until then, keep laughing, keep dreaming, and remember – sometimes, the quirkiest creatures make the best friends.

The End!

INDEX OF DANDY AHURUONYE'S WORKS

Long Search for Greener Pastures – 2014
Waka – 2014
Zinzie – 2015
The Two Grandpas – 2016
Illustrated Children's Bedtime Stories – 2017
Groccolli – 2017
THE SHOEMAKER:
Principles & Guide for Professionals – 2018
DESIGNER'S FINGER:
A Practical Guide for Shoe Professionals – 2019
A Fish Hook and The Riverboy – 2020
A Quiet Duck and The Noisy Chicken – 2020
A Tiny Kingdom of Invisible People – 2020
The Cute Children of Madugascar – 2020
THE WHISPERING POET:
An Anthology of Igbo & Other Proverbs – 2021
Groccofly – 2022
The Adventures of Groccolli – 2022
Nora Never Gave Up – 2022
Reading Glasses for Lady Eagle – 2022
The Eel and Phil in Keel – 2022
The Good and Ugly Weather Friends – 2022
The Grass Fart in Donegal Bay – 2022
The Secrets in my Phlegm - 2022
Positive Brainwash – 2022
Gratitude Journal – 2022
The Power of Gratitude – 2022
My Dogbook – 2022
Meditation Diary – 2022

CREEPERELLA AND THE NINE MISCHIEVOUS MONSTERS

Happyville – 2023
Stinky and The Dung Beetle – 2023
Oh, What A Mars! 2023
The Gull Who Must Be Obeyed – 2023
The Groccolli PictureLand ChatBook – 2023
Trillion-Her – 2023
Finding Love in Cahersiveen – 2023
Lagos Teens and The Marketplace of Dreams – 2023
The Eel, The Duck, and The Groccolli Ring of Love – 2023
Why Did the Wasp Come? – 2023
Roosta & Henn: The Rise of AI Robots – 2023
Lower – 2023
Dodo Returns – 2024
Pet Paradise – 2024
Nightlife Of Mannequins – 2024
HISTORY TREE and The Wrinkles of Time – 2024
Dandy Ahuruonye's Fridge of Secrets – 2024
The Extraordinary World of Ordinary Objects – 2024
Dandy Ahuruonye's Cheeky Periwinkles – 2024
The Hibernuats: A Tale of Human Hibernation – 2024
The Hungry Alien from Planet Zog – 2024
THE TIME BANK and the Lost Tick-Tock Moments – 2024
A Good Rat – 2024
  Grass Fart in Donegal Bay (Revised) – 2024
  Dandy Ahuruonye's Emoji Kingdom – 2024

A *Fish Hook and The Riverboy (Revised) – 2024*
  Eldoria and the Urban Explorers Club – 2024
The Quiet Duck and a Noisy Chicken – 2024
Dandy Ahuruonye's Gadget Gang – 2024

CREEPERELLA
And
THE NINE MISCHIEVOUS MONSTERS
Dandy Ahuruonye

CREEPERELLA AND THE NINE MISCHIEVOUS MONSTERS

Copyright © 2024 Dandy Ahaoma Ahuruonye

UK | USA | Canada. |Ireland | Australia | India. |New Zealand | South Africa | Japan | China | Nigeria
De Juvenyles is part of the dandyahuruontebooks.com group whose details can be found at
https://dandyahuruonye.wordpress.com & https://www.amazon.com/author/dandyahuruonye
dandyahuruonyebooks
Tallaght, Dublin, Ireland

CREEPERELLA AND THE NINE MISCHIEVOUS MONSTERS

Don't miss out!

Visit the website below and you can sign up to receive emails whenever Dandy Ahuruonye publishes a new book. There's no charge and no obligation.

https://books2read.com/r/B-A-YNSQ-EPGDF

BOOKS 2 READ

Connecting independent readers to independent writers.

Milton Keynes UK
Ingram Content Group UK Ltd.
UKHW042002281024
450365UK00003B/114